Time Change

A Nina Bannister Mystery

by

T'Gracie and Joe Reese

Copyright © 2016 by T'Gracie and Joe Reese

For information, email Cozy Cat Press, cozycatpress@aol.com or visit our website at: www.cozycatpress.com

COZY CAT
PRESS

ISBN: 978-1-939816-84-9
Printed in the United States of America

Cover design by Paula Ellenberger
www.paulaellenberger.com

10 9 8 7 6 5 4 3 2 1

To Robert Louis Stevenson
Who wrote among numerous other works *Treasure Island* and *Kidnapped*, two of Nina Bannister's favorites

Fort Massachusetts is a fort on West Ship Island along the Mississippi Gulf Coast of the United States. It was built following the War of 1812, with brick walls during 1859-1866, and remained in use until 1903.

PROLOGUE: A FEW MOMENTS WITH A YOUNG ATTORNEY

The May morning was like cream. It swirled, white and viscous, in the otherwise dark coffee that was the universe, and it begged to be savored by everyone but especially by the young.

And so the young woman savored it as she opened the door of her battered Volkswagen and got out, stretching for a moment, listening to the ocean which was no more than half a mile distant, and letting her eyes scan the town around her.

Bay St. Lucy, a little kaleidoscope Mississippi village on the Gulf Coast. Red board building here, bright blue shack there, lighthouse in the distance, dog over by the fire plug, squirrel in the tree—all there in front of her, above her, surrounding her, just waiting to be gobbled up by her senses and devoured by her beingness.

She checked her watch: twelve fifteen.

She had, due to the grace of a principal who didn't understand coffee and cream and young love—but had been partially persuaded that such things existed—forty-five more minutes.

And so she slammed shut the door of the car with somewhat more force than might have been absolutely necessary, causing, as it did, the entire vehicle to shudder somewhat. Then she strode off across Sea Horse Avenue.

Soon the ramshackle building she'd been approaching stood before her, the step-up porch beneath her, the buzzer at hand, and the click-lock negotiated.

Raaack!

The door swung open.

A narrow staircase was still musty as she ascended it, and she knew that it would always be musty until it was torn down, and that the hours the two of them had spent washing it out had been absolutely wasted. But that did not matter. It was their staircase, their dark brown and ragged carpet, their pictures hung on the walls above the hand railings, their dim yellow buzzing and precarious lights hanging from the ceiling, and their door at the top of the stairway which now was opening, to reveal a tall young mop-haired man in a shirt that was as not quite right as the entrance stairwell itself.

"Hey!" this young man shouted, his face illuminating like a fall carnival on a Friday night.

"Hey!" she responded, a bit softly due to her being low on breath—for she was on the eighth step now, two more to go—"How's the morning? Are we rich and famous yet?"

"Give me until this afternoon!"

"You keep saying that. I'm disappointed."

"So no hug?"

"I didn't say that."

And then they were, deliciously, embracing.

Which they did for far too long, given the forty-three minutes and twelve—now eleven now ten now nine seconds they still had to be together before she returned to the high school.

But at the end, they unembraced, and that was not too bad either, for they were now standing at arm's length from each other, with just the right spacing so that she could look up at him—she was short and he was tall—and say:

"I love you, Frank Bannister."
"I love you, Nina Bannister. So let's have lunch!"
And they did.

CHAPTER ONE: BREAKFAST OF CHAMPIONS

They ate in a corner of the office, sitting on opposite sides of a small table and basking in sunlight that poured in through a large window on the east side of the building. The roofs of Bay St. Lucy lay spread below them, and, farther beyond, they could see a silver-blue and glistening strip of color that was the ocean.

And it was a perfect spring morning in the year 1969.

"Mmmm," said Nina, "where did you get fresh croissants and chicken salad?"

Her husband of eight months smiled, making him look, she remarked to herself, even more like Jimmy Stewart.

"A new place. Just opened up on B St. and 8th Avenue. Italian. I heard people talking about it earlier on this morning."

"Name?" Nina took a big bite of her sandwich, showering the plate with an explosion of croissant flake crumbs.

"Bag of something or other."

"Bag of? That doesn't make any sense."

"Well, you know the Italians. Bagatelli's I think it is."

Frank had a smear of chicken salad in the corner of his mouth and Nina reached across, wiped it away with her finger and popped it into her mouth.

"Well, this is wonderful, whatever their name is."

"It was the best I could do. Sorry it's not fish sticks and tater tots."

"I'll make the sacrifice if it lets me eat lunch with Jimmy Stewart. I mean the Jimmy Stewart in *Mr. Smith Goes to Washington*, not the old raspy Jimmy Stewart."

"Okay, I'll be Jimmy Stewart if you'll be June Allyson."

"She's too goody- goody."

"And what are you, the vampire woman?"

"I have my dark side."

He smiled:

"If we had a double cot up here, maybe you could show me that dark side."

"Not enough time, not between fourth and fifth periods anyway. And besides, what if a prospective client walked in?"

"Could only help. What would you think if you were looking around for a lawyer, and you found one having sex in the corner of his office?"

"Hire him on the spot." She crunched a potato chip.

"Damned straight. So now that we've got that settled, maybe we could just use the carpet. At least until I can get some cots in here."

"Nope. I'm not in the mood. Teaching *Beowulf*. Now if we were doing *Lady Chatterley's Lover*…"

"That's the dirty one, isn't it?"

"They're all dirty. You just have to know how to read them."

"So this is what draws people to become English teachers."

"Yep, sex and the big bucks. So really, tell me Frank—how did the morning go?"

"A little slow."

"Which means?"

"I did *The New York Times* crossword puzzle." He nodded his head toward a fold of newspaper and pen on the kitchen counter.

"All of it?"

"No, but a couple of answers in the upper left quadrant. And I've still got the afternoon ahead of me."

"So do the dumb old crossword if you want; but I have a much better use for your time."

"And that would be?"

"Think up baby names."

"Aha! So you're…"

"No, no, no, not yet. But it will happen."

"Lord knows we're trying."

"Yes we are. And I think I've come up with two names, one for a girl and one for a boy."

"Well, whenever it comes, it should be one of those."

"Yes, it should."

"And the names are?"

"Pearl if it's a girl, and Furl if it's a boy."

"Pearl and Furl? I don't know, Nina, those are just so common. You hear them all the time. Mary and William, Susan and Thomas, Pearl and Furl. Can't you be a little more creative?"

"Okay, I'm working on it. So what do you want to do tonight, Frank?"

"I thought we'd have an elegant dinner somewhere. Maybe pheasant under glass, with champagne cocktail to start and a fine Chablis during the meal."

"Or we could have tuna fish on rye with one can apiece of Blatz Beer."

"Better still. As long as we can have mad, passionate, stink-sweating sex afterward."

"I was thinking more of Scrabble."

"Aha! There's that dark side again."

"Yes, it never disappears entirely. But enough dirty talk, I have to go and teach the youth of our city."

"And I have to stay here and defend the criminals of our city."

She rose, and moved their now empty plates to the kitchen counter, saying:

"I wish there were some."

"Me too," he added, accompanying her to the door. "It's the most disgustingly law-abiding little hard-scrabble village I've ever seen. People here don't even get divorced."

"Well, you could've started your practice in one of the big cities of the world, where crime is rampant. Chicago, for example."

"Nope. This is where you and I grew up, Nina, and it suits us. Now go and do your thing with Baying Wolf."

"*Beowulf.*"

"Whatever. But when you get to *Lady Chatterley's Lover*, let me know."

"You'll be the first."

"Bye, baby."

"Bye, James Stewart."

And, with visions of a black and white Frank Bannister filibustering in Washington rather than a colorized Frank Bannister doing the *New York Times* crossword puzzle in Bay St. Lucy, she returned to the high school.

The Volkswagen ride back was a time for musing. She negotiated the sleepy and tangled streets while wondering how long she'd have to be a teacher. Not long, certainly. Not that she hated it. She had a rapport with her students, and had possessed that closeness from the first time she entered a classroom. Some people, despite all of the education classes in the world, were simply ineffective, boring, teachers. There were several who taught with her now, a few who'd even taught her when she was a student. They knew their subjects well enough, but they were dreadfully dreadfully horribly despicably forever and forever and forever amen boring.

Which she was not.

Teaching was fun for her, and it became in turn fun for her students.

It pleased her secretly every time she had to stop some discussion or some group activity by announcing:

"All right; the period is over. You've got to go to your next class!"

And they were dumbstruck, wondering where the time had gone.

No, there was something definitely enjoyable about that.

But the halls, the drab halls, the huge boys hurling themselves against the lockers, the fire drills, the constant grade reports and attendance reports and parent conferences and fish sticks and spinach and more fish sticks and, "Can I have your tartar sauce?"

And the principal.

Old Ms. Wickersley.

She thought about Frank's complaint: no crime in Bay St. Lucy.

Well, perhaps someone could kill old Ms. Wickersley.

What a wonderful thought!

And there were so many ways it could be done!

She'd run through half a dozen in her mind when the main high school building appeared before her, and with a vision of what her life would certainly be like. Certainly certainly certainly she would teach for a year or perhaps two depending on the law practice. But that practice would invariably prosper. Frank was too smart, too hard working, too well-liked here in this little village that had always been home to both of them.

Within a year he'd be making enough to support them, this she knew.

And within a year she'd be pregnant.

She could almost feel life growing within her now. Chemically, physically, no. No, it had not yet happened.

But they'd been trying only a few scant months.

By the end of the summer she and Frank and God would have worked together and be producing her first child.

This she knew.

She parked the car, got out, slung her purse over her shoulder, negotiated the parking lot, went in through the main entrance, avoided being run over by two of the coaches, said hello to two of the secretaries, and was halfway down the hall and within sight of her home room when she heard:

"Mrs. Bannister!"

Adelia Wickersley.

Damn.

Double damn.

"Mrs. Bannister, could I please see you in my office?"

This she knew: she would never never never never under ANY circumstances, become a principal.

Even if she herself were to become a good principal, the vision and memory of Adelia Wickersley would haunt her psyche forever, and she would wander the colorless halls wondering, "Have I become like her? Have I, thinking all along that I'm Nina Bannister, secretly become Nina Wickersley?"

With immense self- discipline, she forced herself to turn.

There, standing like the Wicked Witch of the East but shorter—although equally green—was Adelia Wickersley. The distance between the two women (actually one woman and one other kind of creature) was no more than fifteen feet.

A small handgun, taken from her purse, and fired twice, right toward the belly.

The hall was crowded; who would notice?

Who would care?

Hitler had almost been assassinated by his own generals. What was the difference?

"Yes, Mrs. Wickersley?"

"I need to speak to you right now."

"Yes, ma'am."

She might as well have been a student. In fact, as she walked toward the principal's office—the principal herself having disappeared behind the door—she realized that she was always getting in much more trouble as a teacher than she'd ever gotten into as a student.

Trying to make sense of this conundrum, she walked into the office, and found Principal Wickersley seated behind her mammoth wood-of-some-kind desk, staring up at her. Nina sniffed and gave a little cough. The office reeked of Eau de Lavender; Principal Wickersley must bathe it it.

No, this was not the Wicked Witch of the East. In comparison to this woman, the Wicked Witch of the East was Lucille Ball. This woman's face had been shrunken and pruned by the constant hatred she must have felt toward the outside world. With lava gray hair and REDREDRED lipstick, she resembled an erupting volcano, except not nearly as much fun, and much more dangerous.

"Sit down, please."

"Yes, ma'am."

The only good thing was, Nina realized, that she did not have to search for words. Two were all she needed, and those two she'd just said and would continue to repeat until she was dismissed, feeling as guilty as—no matter why she'd been called in here—a child molester or a presidential assassin.

Adelia Wickersley heaved a huge sigh, giving Nina, as she did so, a chance to study her face. Thousands and thousands of wrinkles. Not smile wrinkles—all frown wrinkles, and wrinkles that called to mind the scarred face of a lunar landscape.

The sigh oozed out of her mouth and died somewhere over the table, leaving arid and dead space into which were poured the poisonous words:

"It's your student again, Ms. Bannister."

Oh God.

Nina wished once more for the gun, only a small handgun, any sort of a weapon really, but this time she would use it on herself.

"Which student?"

For she had over a hundred in five classes of English.

But really there was no need to ask, a point the principal underscored by asking:

"Do you need to ask?"

Now Nina sighed, but her sigh was a theatrical failure, a joke really, compared to the sigh which had preceded it.

"No, I guess not. You're talking about Penelope."

"About Miss Royale, yes."

"I guess, technically, she's not only *my* student."

"She is *your* home room student."

"Yes. She is that."

Don't ask what's she done don't ask what's she done don't ask what's she done don't ask what's she done don't ask what she's done don't ask what's she done don't ask what's she done don't ask what she's done don't ask what's she done don't ask what's she done don't ask what she's done don't ask what's she done—

"What's she done?"

"We're waiting to hear about that."

"You don't know what she's done?"

"We don't know what the police are choosing to call it."

"Oh my God."

"Perhaps we can avoid taking the Lord's name in vain?"

"I'm sorry."

"And, besides, we get quite enough profanity from Miss Royale." Principal Wickersley frowned and her wrinkles shifted downward.

"Yes, I know. Penn and I are working to raise her vocabulary."

"I see. Well, at any rate, I've found a substitute for your fifth period class."

"A substitute?" Nina shifted in her chair. Dust motes danced in the sunlight around Principal Wickersley's head.

"Yes, Mrs. Johnson has agreed to take over the class."

"While I—"

"While you drive into town and visit Miss Royale."

"Who is—"

"At the police station."

"I should probably have guessed that."

"Yes, you should have. The good thing is we have only one student at the police station and none at the hospital. Or at the morgue."

"Who did she hurt?"

"Do you mean, 'Whom did she hurt?'" Principal Wickersley leaned forward in her chair and her eyes razored into Nina's.

"That's exactly what I meant to say. Whom did she hurt and how many and how bad?"

"Football players, two; they may miss some of the spring training workouts."

"And why did she hurt them?"

"In order to answer that question appropriately, Mrs. Bannister, I should be forced to employ the phrase which you yourself have just used, and which should not be used, at least not in a school or in a church."

"I understand."

"But, Mrs. Bannister, you also should understand something else. You have apparently created a strong bond with Miss Royale. Before being taken away she insisted on speaking with you. You were not, unfortunately, here. I realize that you are newly married, and wish to have lunch with your husband. But you on your part should realize that we are teachers for the duration of the entire school day, during the course of which many things may happen. Even during lunch, which is when this unfortunate event took place. In the future, therefore, I must insist—"

"I know. I'll have lunch in the cafeteria. And I'll go downtown now and talk to Penn."

"Thank you, Mrs. Bannister. And now I believe it's time for the bell."

Nina rose and left the room, cursing softly and ineffectively. She was very bad at obscenities, only a few of which she actually knew, and even these, when uttered in public, elicited laughs.

But she did her best as she approached the office, begged the use of one of the school telephones, and dialed a number.

There was a click, and a familiar voice at the other end.

"Bannister Law Firm."

"You've got a client."

"What?"

"You've got a client. Meet me at the city jail in fifteen minutes."

"I don't know who you are, but you must have a wrong number."

"Don't try to be funny, Frank. Something's happened. One of my students needs your help."

"You sound a lot like Nina, I'll give you that. Now come on, who are you, really?"

"Fifteen minutes. Good bye."

She hung up, left the building, got back into her car, and drove to the jail.

She arrived there just as Frank did, and she watched him chain his blue bicycle to the rack in front of the red brick building while she got out of her car.

They met in front of the main entrance and exchanged a quick hug.

"So what," he asked, "is going on?"

"I'm not sure. I've got a student in trouble."

"What student? What trouble?"

"Girl. Assault."

"A girl was assaulted?"

"Are you kidding me?"

"I don't understand."

"It's Penelope Royale. Penn."

"Oh. This is the girl you've talked about." Frank pulled open the glass door.

"Yes, she's in my home room. For some reason, she likes me. But she's got real problems. Single-parent child. Her mother's gone half the time, nobody seems to know where. There's been talk of sending her away to some kind of foster care center." She entered the anteroom with Frank at her heels.

"You sure that would be bad?"

"Of course, it would be bad. She lives here, she goes to school here. She and her mother only came to Bay St. Lucy a year or so ago, but she's still one of us."

"All right, so what do you want me to do about this situation?"

"Talk to the sheriff."

"And tell him?"

"The right things. Make this go away, Frank." Nina stopped at the high counter and reached for the clipboard to sign in.

"You may underestimate me as a lawyer." Frank scrawled and added his name to the clipboard.

"Well, your image does suffer a little because of the bicycle."

"It does not. Now if it was a girl's bike—"

"Perry Mason never rode a bike to court."

"That may be, but I may not have to ride one much longer either."

"What are you talking about?"

"Something just happened."

"When?"

"Maybe an hour ago."

"I know something happened an hour ago. Penn Royale beat up Bay St. Lucy's offensive line."

"Something else happened."

"What?"

"We got an invitation to dinner."

"Well, I guess that's nice. But I had my mouth set for tuna fish."

"You may not get it. Not at this dinner, anyway."

"So who invited us?"

Frank, though, merely nodded toward the door behind the counter and said:

"Tell you later. Let's go in. You talk to your student, I'll talk to the sheriff and see what I can do."

They entered.

There was a tangle of corridors and sickly green paint, and there were desks everywhere. Typing rattled like machine gun fire, and people in various kinds of uniforms ran here and there, looking by turns serious and confused, occupied and idle. At the first hallway, Frank was led away from her, and she found herself being led into the innards of the building by a squat curly-headed young man.

He turned after a few paces down still another hallway and smiled:

"You Mrs. Bannister?"

"Yes, I am."

The smile broadened. She liked him.

He was the anti-Adele Wickersley.

"I just been hired on here as deputy. Name is Moon Rivard."

She took his hand:

"Nice to meet you, Officer Rivard."

"Moon be better if you don't mind."

"Moon it is then. And I'm Nina."

"All right then, Miss Nina."

"You aren't from Bay St. Lucy?"

"New Iberia. Cajun through and through. But I heard they was an opening over here and, well, here I am."

"We're happy to have you. Now, about Penn—"

"You mean Miss Royale?"

"Yes."

"Back here in one of the holding cells. We didn't put her in with nobody else, fearin' as we did for their safety."

"*Their* safety?"

"Yes, ma'am. This Miss Royale needs a much tougher prison environment than what we got ourselves here."

"All right, I think I understand. Take me to her."

"Just you come right this way."

He led further into the labyrinth that was Bay St. Lucy's jail, until, turning a corner, Nina saw Penelope Royale.

She was sitting on what seemed a kind of army cot. She had on a t-shirt and blue jeans, and she was staring at the cinder block wall behind the cot.

"Penn!"

She turned upon hearing Nina's voice, and a weak smile spread across her face.

The smile was, thought Nina, the only thing about Penelope Royale that was weak. She was not a tall girl, perhaps five feet six or so, but she was unbelievably muscular, and the tight fitting t-shirt allowed every flex and bulge to stand out even more clearly.

"Mrs. Bannister!"

"Penn, are you all right?"

"Yes, ma'am. I'm sorry, ma'am."

"Well, I'm sorry too. Everybody's sorry."

"It's just—when they started saying those things—"

For the first time Nina noticed that the metal door of the cell was ajar.

"At least they haven't locked you up."

"No, ma'am. I don't know what they want to do with me."

"Frank is here. Maybe he can help."

"Your husband, the lawyer?"

"Yes."

Penn frowned. "I don't think I can afford a lawyer, Ms. Bannister."

"You can't afford not to have a lawyer. Here, let me come in." The jail cell was cooler than the corridor and Nina felt goose-bumpy.

Nina entered and rubbed her bare arms up and down to warm up. She found a chair in the corner of the cell. She sat down, sighed, and finally asked:

"So what happened?"

Penelope shrugged her muscular shoulders and mumbled:

"Those g——m——! When they h——, I just couldn't k——my s——any longer."

"Penn, your language."

"I know."

It was, Nina could not help noting, truly remarkable language. Colorful, vibrant, imaginative, and effective. She herself would have liked, if truth be known, to have borrowed some of Penelope's vocabulary to deal with Adelia Wickersley.

But of course, it was inappropriate and the two of them would have to work together to clean it up.

Still, surely it belonged somewhere.

Perhaps she'd write a novel someday, and Penelope could be a part of it.

First though there was the matter of getting her out of jail.

"Now try again girl. What happened?"

A sigh, and the voice—softer than one might have imagined, given that it came from the near destroyer of two middle linebackers—rumbling:

"Some of the football players."

"Where did it happen?"

"In the hall, after third period. I was getting some things out of my locker. They got around me and were saying things. They do that sometimes."

"I know. I know, Penn."

"It was worse today though."

"Things about your mother Eva?"

"Yeah. It's always that. It used to be about me, and how I look. Now they've learned they can pick on Mom. You know, Mrs. Bannister, Mom has to work at night. Sometimes it's real late when she gets in."

And sometimes, Nina had learned—for good teachers make it their business to learn such things— she didn't come in at all.

"They were calling her a—they said she was a—"

"Shh. Don't worry about it. I understand. I know what they were saying, and I know it isn't true."

"Mom isn't the best all the time, but after Dad left us—"

"Sure."

"She tries hard, you know?"

"Of course, she does."

"And then these two f——think they have to——about her——!"

"Penn!"

"Sorry."

"Just say, 'these two thoughtless and immature young men'."

"All right. That. For these two—"

"Or don't say anything at all."

Penn did not, thought Nina, probably because she was almost ready to break out into tears.

She did not do so, in part because of the arrival of Frank, along with the young man who'd just introduced himself as Moon Rivard.

"Miss Royale," the young man said, "you got another visitor. This here's Mr. Bannister. He's a lawyer."

"Hello, Penelope."

"Hello, sir."

"You're in a little trouble, or so it seems."

"Yes, Mr. Bannister."

Moon Rivard smiled:

"The ones dat was in trouble was them two football players."

"How badly," Nina asked, "were they hurt?"

Moon Rivard shook his head:

"One of 'em might lose a tooth, and they checking on the other one's ribs, see if any of them might be broke."

"They're not," said Frank quietly, "going to press any charges."

Moon laughed at this.

"Too ashamed. Get beat up by a girl!"

"Penn," said Nina, "is testimony to the fact that women are not always the weaker sex."

To which Penelope mumbled:

"Those e——, g——,l——s."

"Penn!"

"Sorry."

"What did we decide to call them?"

The soft voice, scarcely audible:

"Those immature young men."

Moon Rivard:

"Me I liked what she said first better."

Nina glared at him:

"That is *not* helping, Mr. Rivard!"

"Sorry."

Frank stepped forward and said to Penelope:

"I think you're in luck this time, Miss Royale. I've just talked to the sheriff. No one wants anything more made of this than has already happened. He's willing to release you in my charge. Mine and Nina's."

"What does that mean, sir?"

"We're kind of—well, responsible for you."

"Responsible?"

Nina spoke up:

"It just means that maybe you and I can spend some time together, Penelope."

"Time? Doing what?"

Nina thought about saying *crocheting*, but also almost broke out laughing at the thought.

Finally, in desperation, she said:

"Fishing."

"What?"

"Let's go fishing together. Ever fished? I mean, real fishing, in the Gulf?"

"No, ma'am."

"Well, I have. And I know Lazarus Cousins, who owns a fishing boat. It's called The *Sea Turtle*. Mr. Cousins was a friend of my father's, and the two of them used to take me out deep sea fishing. I'll call him tonight. If he doesn't have a party scheduled, maybe he can take us out after school tomorrow."

"I don't want to be trouble to you, Mrs. Bannister."

"It's no trouble. I haven't fished since Frank and I got married."

"You've had," said Frank, quietly, "other things to do."

"Be quiet."

"Sorry."

"So is that a date, Penn?"

"Yes, ma'am. If you say so."

"I do say so. Except you have to promise: no more fights, and no more bad words."

"All right. I promise."

"The sheriff suggests," said Frank, "that Mr. Rivard take you home now, Penelope. You'll be excused for the rest of the school day. It's almost time for classes to be over anyway."

"I don't have any money to pay you, Mr. Bannister."

"Catch a big fish tomorrow, and give it to us."

To which Penelope Royale smiled.

It was her first smile, Nina surmised, in quite some time.

Within five minutes, Nina was standing in the parking lot, watching Frank unlock the chain to his bicycle.

"Well, Mr. Mason, I'd say you did pretty well in there."

"I had other forces on my side."

"Such as?"

"The coaches. They'd never live it down if it got out that two of their star players got beat up by–"

"—by a girl, I know."

"She is, I will say, quite a girl."

"That she is."

"Well, at any rate, Nina, you're responsible for her now."

"*I* am! What about you?"

"I don't know the first thing about fishing."

"Coward!"

"You've got that right. Oh, but there is this other thing I was telling you about."

"The dinner, you mean?"

"I certainly do."

"Okay, so we're invited to dinner. So what?"

"It's who invited us that answers the *so what* question."

"I'll keep biting. Who invited us?"

"At about ten this morning a black limo pulled into our parking lot."

"A black car invited us to dinner? Where're we going to eat, a garage?"

"Hush."

"I'll hush, but you might want to get on with this story sometime before Christmas."

"A few minutes later a guy in a uniform was knocking at my door."

"And you got up from doing the crossword puzzle and you pushed the chair back and you stood up and you took one step toward the door and then another step and then—"

"—and finally I got to the door, opened it, and took this note which was handed to me by the chauffeur."

"The chauffeur? Who has a chauffeur?"

"This guy. Read it."

So saying, Frank produced from his pocket an elegant letter, on which was written:

MR. FRANK BANNISTER
BARRISTER
DEAR SIR;

YOU AND YOUR WIFE ARE CORDIALLY INVITED
SATURDAY, May 14, 1969
8:00 PM
TO DINNER
2255 BREAKERS BOULEVARD
HOMER BARON ROBINSON

For a time, Nina could do nothing except stare at the note.

"We're going to the old Robinson mansion?"

"So it would seem."

"Frank, I've never even been within two hundred yards of that place. And I nod to Mrs. Robinson when I see her on the street, but—"

"But you don't see her on the street much, because she's in a limousine. Or she's at home, and her maids are shopping."

"Frank, we don't belong with these kind of people! Homer Robinson's one of the richest people in—"

"The universe. Or so people say. As though they knew anything about him, which they don't."

"What they do know is, he controls everything in this town. Word is that even the school board won't do a thing until he agrees to it. So what does he want with us?"

Frank shrugged.

Then he smiled and said with his best Jimmy Stewart drawl:

"Well, I think maybe—maybe he needs a lawyer!"

"You're getting better at that imitation."

"The imitation of Jimmy Stewart or the imitation of a lawyer?"

Nina was unable to answer the question, because she was kissing her husband.

CHAPTER TWO: TO CATCH A WHALE

Nina watched as the buildings and ships of Bay St.
Lucy got smaller and smaller. There were walls on
either side of them for a time, the long concrete jetties
that bordered the ship channel. But then those
disappeared and the ocean subsumed them. It was the
deepest blue she could imagine, except when the sun
went behind a cloud, and then it would magically turn
to green, always a water blanket rising and falling, the
waves never too high, not breaking into whitecaps now,
but simply thicker, deeper, on and on as far as she could
see.

Finally, even the faint buildings on the shore
disappeared.

And there was nothing on either side but water.

Nina could hear Lazarus Cousins singing in the
cabin:

"Oh well and a-day, to you fair Spanish ladies
Well and a-day to you ladies of Spain,
For the captain's decided we sail at the morning,
And so never more will we see ye again!"

Finally he let the engine slow, then idle.

The boat rocked easily in a light swell.

Lazarus Cousins was loved by everyone in Bay St.
Lucy, most of whom had gone fishing with him at one
time or another. The fact that he charged lower rates
than other operators made them overlook the fact that
he was black, which they would have overlooked

anyway, because his parties always caught fish. Tall, gaunt, wrinkle-bearded and sparkling-eyed, he faced the world through eyes as bright as the sea he fished in. Nina couldn't remember a time when she hadn't known him, and she'd always idolized him much as she'd idolized her father. Somehow, too, she sensed that Penelope had begun to feel the same way about him, for the girl had been looking at everything on the boat with what seemed a sense of wonder ever since the two of them had boarded, more than half an hour ago.

"Awright, y'all fisherfolk come on down here into the hold. Want y'all to look at something."

"What is it?" asked Nina.

"Just come along down, that's right!"

Within a few seconds, the three of them had descended the six steps that led down to the small cabin Cousins called his hold and were bending over what seemed an inverted television.

"What *is* this thing?" asked Penn.

"Radar."

"L——d!"

"Penn!"

"Sorry. Look—what's that green blob of a thing?"

"Kelp bed likely as anything. Kelp's a kind of seaweed."

"What about the black shadows passing over the blob?"

"Fish, Miss Royale."

"What kind do you think?"

"Me, I guess sea bass. Tolerable chance of redfish, hard to be sure. Anyway, they's a school of them down there, right below us about thirty feet down."

"How big are they?"

Cousins shrugged:

"Some they get up fifteen pounds, maybe two feet long. They some sharks down there though that measure up ten feet."

"Wow!"

"Hey, Miss Nina, think you ready to make youself useful now?"

"Sure," Nina answered. "What do you need?"

"How 'bout baitin' a rig? Mullet in the bait buckets up toward the prow."

Nina rose, made her way toward the front of the vessel and spied the rod and reel she was to prepare as well as several ice-filled five-gallon buckets labeled *bait*. In two minutes, all was ready. She found herself at the stern of the boat, ready to hand the baited rod to Penn.

"Ready to get buckled in?"

"You sure you want me to go first, Mrs. Bannister?"

"Of course. That's why we're out here, so you can learn to fish."

"I don't know, I just never…"

"Stop talking and let's get this belt around you."

Penelope smiled weakly and took the rod.

Within a few seconds, she was buckled into the fishing chair.

"Now, to cast, you press down on this little button and hold it while you rear back like you were getting ready to throw a baseball."

"Like this?"

"Atta girl! Now throw it as hard as you can, but hold tight to the rod's handle, and let up on the button just as you start your throw!"

"Okay, here goes!"

She hurled the line, and Nina could see the mullet-bait sparkling against the sunlight as it went flying a good sixty feet over the ocean.

Plop.

Into the water.

"Great cast!"

"Really?"

"Of course! Penn, you're strong enough to beat up football players, you're certainly strong enough to cast a baitfish!"

"Are we fishing?" asked Lazarus Cousins from the cabin.

"We're fishing!" answered Nina.

"Okay, we' gonna troll a little, just so mister bait is movin' in the water when it get down neighborhood of the fish. Nina, you best show her how to let the line run. Best is to let about fifty yards out before we tell the reel he got to stop spinnin'."

Nina did as she was told, and the reel spindled monotonously as line disappeared into the waves. From the cabin came Cousins' voice, which mixed with the soft growling of the waves:

"Fifteen men on the dead man's chest—

Yo ho ho and a bottle of rum!

Drink and the devil had done for the rest!

"Yo ho ho and a bottle of rum!"

After slightly more than five minutes, Penelope got her first bite.

The line snapped tight, pulling the tip of the reel downward as the reel buzzed.

"Penn!" cried Nina. "Penn, pull back!"

The girl did nothing for an instant, and the nearly invisible spot where line disappeared into blue-green water receded.

"Pull back—and flip the drag switch!"

Finally, the panic left Penn's eyes and she jerked hard-upward, her finger snapping the gleaming little silver handle that froze the reel.

"You've got him, he's hooked!" screamed Nina, putting both of her palms down on Penn's shoulders. "Reel in! Reel in!"

"Okay, here goes!"

She pulled back on the line with all her strength, and then began reeling.

"Get him, Penelope!" yelled Nina, attempting to estimate, by the slow turning of the reel and the equally slow approach to the boat of the telltale spot where line entered water, just what might have been on the other end.

Penn's face continued to be a mixture of shock and delight, as she squinted into the sun, pursed her lips, held onto the rod's handle like death with her left hand, and laboriously turned the reel crank with her right.

"What is it?" she screamed.

"Redfish! Sucker's right at the top of the water!" responded Lazarus Cousins from the prow. "Good size, big fella!!"

"He's getting closer to the boat, Penn! You're getting him!"

"I know! I can feel him coming!"

Suddenly, they saw two other objects enter the scene. These were dark brown objects that seemed to be tearing at the mass of red.

"Damn," hissed Cousins, almost under his breath.

"What are those things?" shouted Penelope.

"Sharks. Dog sharks. They tryin' to steal our redfish!"

"What can we do about them?"

"This!"

He opened a compartment in the side of the boat. Then he reached in and pulled out a handgun, which gleamed oily-metal against the huge orange disc that was the rising sun.

"Now watch what ol' Lazarus does to thieves!"

BLAM!

BLAM!

The water exploded in two volcanic atom bomb blasts of sea spray, shark meat, and brown kelp, which rained back down on the otherwise calm bay surface.

"Thas' better," growled Cousins, putting the gun away.

Penelope's eyes were like saucers, and, quietly but with obvious wonder in her voice, she said:

"I never t——a —— in my —— g—— life!"

"Penn!"

"Sorry! But that was amazing! I *love* fishing! Mr. Cousins?"

"Yes, miss?"

"You got any other guns aboard?"

He nodded and smiled grimly:

"A twelve gauge."

"What do you use that for?"

"Bigger sharks. And pirates. Now come on, you catch that fish!"

"You got it!"

Penelope began reeling faster now, and Nina realized that Lazarus Cousins had started the engine and was chugging forward, pulling the fish along with the boat.

"Look," she shouted, pointing at the line as it entered the water, the disappearing-point now beginning to circle slowly, "He's tiring out! Just keep at it!"

This kept on for perhaps a minute, with Nina running from one side of the chair to another and shouting bits of useless advice, useless because there were only two things for Penn to do—hold on and reel—and she was doing both quite well, the smile on her face broadening as she did so.

Finally there was a miniature explosion in the water ten feet or so from the side of the boat, and the ocean flashed red.

"There he is, Penn"

"I KNOW I KNOW!"

Within a minute, Lazarus Cousins was standing at the stern of the boat, extending out over the water a ten foot aluminum rod with a net on the end.

"Just keep fighting him, girl! Bring him this way a little more! Keep him coming! Almost—THERE!"

And with one final lunge, the captain netted the glistening redfish, then lifted him over the stern rail.

There he was on the floor of the boat, wriggling and thrashing, the line extending from his mouth, with three excited people dancing around him.

The next five minutes provided a spectacle even more thrilling than the catching of the fish had been, for it was during this brief time that *The Old Man of the Sea* showed his stuff. He was a good pilot, a good fishing guide, and a good many other things. But no one in the world was better at dispatching a fish (with a heavy ball peen hammer blow to the head), slitting it open, gutting it, throwing the unwanted entrails into a waste bucket, fileting it, and stashing the two slabs of what could easily be the night's meal for all of them under a thin layer of shaved ice.

And then things returned to the fishing part of the trip, while conversation whirred on, concerning the day's first catch.

Penn:

"How big do you think he is?"

Cousins:

"Eight, maybe ten pounds. Big enough to give you quite a tussle or so it look to me, anyway."

"I'll say! How are you going to cook him, Ms. Bannister?"

"Any way you want, Penn. There are lots of ways to cook redfish. Now come on, let's catch another one!"

"Hold the phone," said Cousins. "We gonna take this Sea Turtle a little more far out. I want to show Miss Penelope Storm Island, and old Fort Massachusetts! She likes shark fish—well, she gonna' be seein' some out there!"

"It's pretty far out, isn't it?" asked Nina.

"It's a barrier island twelve miles off the coast. Didn't I never take you out there?"

"Yes, I love the place."

And she did. She'd been several times to Fort Massachusetts as a child. She loved its massive red brick walls, its Civil War history, and the huge guns atop its parapets.

"We doin' twenty knots. Be out there in half an hour. Don't know I ever tell you, but I used to work for the Park Service. Gave some tours of the place, and then, for a while, ran the ferry that goes out there twice a day. That's when I got wised up about the sharks."

"Sharks?"

"More out there than any place I ever saw. Now let's go!"

They did, and, sure enough, within half an hour the massive fortress rose up over the horizon.

"We gonna' circle around the island," said Cousins "Then we moor this ol' boat to the pier on the back side."

They did so, and within five minutes they were walking past a snow cone stand open only on weekends, toward the red-walled structure that formed an inverted capital *D* with its curved portion facing out into the ocean and away from Bay St. Lucy.

It was a slow day, only a few people around, four or five tourists and two employees of the National Park Service. One of these, a smiling young woman, offered to take them on a brief tour, but Cousins declined. This was the kind of thing he loved doing himself, and so for the next half hour he took them through the maze like halls of the structure, showing them the symmetrical arches that supported the roof, and detailing the fort's capture by confederate forces and its recapture scant months later.

Soon they were climbing the central spiral staircase and exiting onto the five-foot-thick wall.

"How tall are these walls, Lazarus?" Nina found herself asking.

Had she not known at one time?

He smiled.

"They was eight feet high during the Civil War, but around the turn of the century the government builded them up higher."

"How high are we above sea level then?"

"The walls are twenty feet high now, and the spot on this barrier island where the fort find itself sticks up ten feet above the ocean. So we right around thirty feet above sea level."

They wandered for a time, enjoying the soft lapping of waves upon Storm Island's beach, talking of this and that, sitting on a bench by one of the huge black Rodman guns that sat atop one of the wall parapets, and eating ham sandwiches that Lazarus had brought out from the boat.

By one o'clock, they'd cast off and were fishing again.

Nina baited a hook again and watched with satisfaction as Penn, a bit more expertly this time, cast into the ocean.

Two minutes later, the line suddenly grew taut, as it had before, and the pole bent.

"There!" Nina shouted. "Get him!"

But Penelope, a quick study, had already jerked hard to fix the hook in the bass's mouth, and was beginning the process of grinding the reel, and pulling the fish in.

"You've got him, Penn! Keep reeling! This one might be bigger than the last. Just keep him coming!"

"I know! From the way he feels, this one…"

And then it happened.

WHAM!

It was as though Penelope had been kicked by a horse into the seatbelt, over which she was now bent double.

Somehow, by some miracle, she held onto the handle of the rod.

For a second Nina thought the bolts holding the fishing chair to the deck would wrench out of their sockets. She moved over behind Penn and grasped the fishing pole. "I'll help!" she cried.

The reel screamed so fast was it whirling.

Then it began to smoke.

"Let the rod go!" Nina found herself shouting. "Penelope, let it go! Just let it go!"

The boat careened around in a tight circle, Cousins trying to steer it one way and something huge, far out in the ocean, pulling it another.

"Penn, just let it go!"

But the girl had become a fishing statue, her eyes dead-locked and squinting, thick cords of muscle in her bare arms rigid, like unbreakable ropes.

The chair was rocking now, while everything else on the boat or in the water churned, smoked, billowed, screeched, or groaned like metal tearing apart.

"Penn, just let it go!"

But Penn screamed back:

"I'VE GOT HIM!"

And Nina somehow knew that this girl would never let it go.

Cousins was with them now, shouting:

"Miss Nina! Grab the bait bucket and tote it over port side!"

"What do I do with it?"

"Lean yourself over the side! Make it plumb damn full with water!"

She did so while Penn continued to hold on, seemingly ignoring smoke that was coming from the spinning reel.

"Pour water on that reel, Miss Nina! Keep pouring or the line gonna' catch fire!"

She poured:

WHOOSH!

Water drenched the chair, Penn, the deck, and everything else within a ten-foot radius.

But, thank God, thought Nina, *the line did not catch fire.*

"Keep it coming!"

In an instant she was back again, and she poured again:

SSSSSSHHHH! A white cloud of steam rose from the reel.

It was as though she had dunked a red hot bar of iron into a barrel of boiling water.

"Just keep that up, Nina. Look! The fish is turning!"

Nina could tell that, not because of how the nearly invisible line looked like over the water, but because the chair had turned a quarter of a clock face and was now letting the line scream out over the back corner of the boat.

Suddenly the line went slack. Nina let go of the pole, wiping her hands on her pants.

In an instant, Cousins had sprung to Penn's side.

"Set the drag, honey, with this button. Here, I got it. Now reel, girl, reel!"

WHAP! With a backslap, Penn knocked the handle of the reel out from the main apparatus so that it was now a six inch long crank. Her eyes narrowed to slits as she whiled the handle, and whirled it and whirled it, all the while sucking slack line off the ocean, tearing it back onto the reel almost as fast as the fish had sucked it off.

"I CAN CATCH HIM! I CAN DO THIS!"

While Nina gripped hard onto her shoulder, grinned, and whispered in her ear:

"YOU GO, GIRL!"

The smoke went away. Now the screaming of the line had stopped, too.

"Nina!"

"Yes, Lazarus!"

"Take yourself inside the cabin. Open the drawer just next to the wheel. You gonna' find a pair of gloves in there. Get 'em out here!"

She did as she was told, finding the cotton work gloves easily and slipping only three times during the trip, lucky, she told herself, not to have broken her neck because of water that now drenched the deck.

"Here!"

"Okay, now, Penn," shouted Cousins, "stop that reelin' for a time! You done flat out great! Let me hold the rod…"

"I CAN GET THAT THING!"

"Certain and sure you can, baby! But you gotta' put on these gloves or that reel gonna' blister your hand."

"All right!"

Penelope did as she was told, putting the gloves on then holding her arms out parallel to the deck and shaking them.

Her skin was drenched.

For that matter, everyone was drenched.

The Captain gave back the reel and spoke quietly:

"Nina, they's a dry rag right on the cushion over near the stern. You fetch it, then clean up some of this water off the deck. We got to be able to stay on our feet."

"Right."

She did as she was told, trying to get as much seawater off the deck as was possible.

Cousins was massaging Penn's neck muscles, watching all the while the dot where line disappeared into water.

"Couple more minutes. Maybe."

"Then what?"

"Then he gonna run like the wind if they was wind under water! When he does that, just let him go!"

But Penn had looked up and was now shouting:

"WHAT KIND OF FISH IS THAT?"

To which Lazarus Cousins could only shake his head.

" Don't know, mate. Wish I did."

'Mate,' Nina mused.

He had called Penn *mate*.

And it sounded natural.

Finally she asked:

"How much line is on that reel?"

"Near about half mile. Took myself a bunch out yesterday, goin' for game fish."

"And you didn't get any."

"Nary a bite."

"Well, I'm no expert," said Nina. "But if you're talking about game fish, just look out there about a quarter mile astern."

"Well, I be damned," said Cousins.

It was the first time since they'd begun to fish that a curse word had been used on board.

And Penelope hadn't been the one to say it.

Could this—fishing—be the cure for Penelope's constant use of profanity?

Of course, in this case, Nina found herself thinking, a strong word might be justified.

For there in the distance, catching a glint from the sun that had heretofore been hidden by a patch of clouds, sticking up from a blue-green weed patch of color in the middle of white froth, a black pipe was extending out of the ocean.

"What *is* that?" whispered Penn, who was still trying to get her breath.

Cousins bent toward her, until his lips were only inches from the girl's right ear.

"They calls that a marlin."

"A what?"

"It's a marlin, Miss Penelope Royale."

"How big is he?"

"Ten feet long if an inch."

Nina had finished swabbing the deck and was craning her eyes, as they all were, to see the dancing and sun glistening sword of the fish before it disappeared beneath the swell.

"Are you kidding me, Lazarus?"

"No."

"How much does he weigh?"

"Meat muscle tongue and snout, half a ton when you gets him out!"

Penn merely said, in a matter of fact way:

"He's mine."

To which Nina and the captain could only laugh, because they knew it was true.

Finally Cousins:

"Now Penelope—when the big devil run again, the reel gonna' start screamin' like ten stuck pigs and the line'll be smokin' just like before. Nothin' to be scared about, just the line going out so fast."

"I understand."

"Good girl. And Miss Nina, just remember, you gotta' keep dousin' water on the line as it come off the reel. If you don't, Penn's gloves will surely as the Good God made the little apples, catch on fire. Are you understanding me?"

"Got it."

"I know you do, I know you do! Pour that ol' water like you been a-doin,' but don't let those fingers of yours get caught between the bail of the reel and the line as it comes off. If you do that, the line gonna' cut off you finger—snip—just take it right off! You never see it no more! Got that?"

"That's a bit graphic for me, but, yes, I've got it."

"All right. Now we gonna' catch this fish! Oh! There he go!"

It was much like the first time, except that Penn had braced for the run and had her feet pressed hard against two silver metal foot-shapes. Still, the reel screamed again like it was a pig being slaughtered in her lap, and wisps of smoke curled up from the line as though matches were being burned beneath it.

Far out in front of them was an explosion of whitewater. They saw again the marlin's sword extending above the waves, making small tight circles in the spray.

Then the line went limp again and both Nina and Cousins screamed:

"REEL! REEL! REEL!"

The commands were useless, because Penn was churning, gasping, shaking, and pouring every inch of her taut powerful body into that one task, that one desperate need to spin a small silver handle faster than the speed of light or sound.

And slowly, slowly, the scene of the battle neared the boat.

Nina somehow lost track of time.

Finally, she asked Lazarus:

"Something I don't understand."

"What is it?"

"We just were using little mullets for bait. I wouldn't have thought a marlin would bother with bait that small."

He merely shook his head:

"Not what happened."

"Then what did happen?"

"Penn had hooked a sea bass, remember?"

"Oh yeah! And the marlin…"

"The marlin went for the bass and swallowed him whole."

Penn's eyes bulged open.

"HE SWALLOWED THAT BASS WHOLE?"

The captain merely nodded.

"A big fish out there, the Lord surely knows he is!"

And so it went on.

Somehow Nina became aware though that the periods of time when Penn was reeling had become longer, and the periods when the fish was running had become shorter.

This meant that the girl was winning the battle, but it also meant that she was working harder and harder.

Finally she cried out:

"I don't know if I can do this much more!"

Cousins grabbed her shoulder:

"You *can* do it! You winning, baby!"

"My arms feel like spaghetti!"

"Just little longer! He be tired too, I promise you!"

"I don't know, I just don't…"

And then Nina saw it.

Not more than twenty feet beyond the stern of the boat, a section of the ocean darkened like an earthquake had churned up a giant vat of purple ink right under the surface.

Then the great fish jumped.

She would never forget the sight.

Its body seemed jewel-encrusted, glowing, shining more colors than she was aware existed.

Its sword, high in the air now, seemed as long as she was.

Its eye was a white basketball with no seams in it.

For an instant it hung there, ten feet out of the water, absolutely motionless.

Then it gave a huge corkscrew twist, arching its back and nose-diving after its sword back into the water.

Spray drenched the boat, which almost capsized in the gigantic wave that followed.

And the marlin was gone.

Penelope sat motionless in the chair. For all the metal statue she'd been during the battle, she now seemed to melt into sweat and seawater.

She reared back her head and moaned:

"Aaaaahhhhh!"

Her whole body glistened wet in the sunlight. Her hair had matted into her eyes, but her hands remained frozen tight around the rod handle.

"Aaaaahhhh! He's gone!"

Nina was beside her now:

"It's all right!"

"I thought I had him!"

"You did, baby! You did have him! You almost won the fight!"

"What a beautiful fish!"

"I know, Penn girl! I know!"

"I wanted him so bad!"

"You fought a brave battle, girl. The bravest I've ever seen. I'll never forget how you fought that fish!"

Then the three of them simply half laughed and half cried for a time, but there was nothing left to say. Penn unfastened the seat belt, and all three of them fell into a people knot in the bottom of the boat.

The smoke from the spinning line had almost completely dissipated now, but it still smelled like the boat was on fire.

Finally, Penn asked:

"What was it?"

The captain shook his head:

"That was a blue marlin, honey. Most fishermen work their whole lives to catch a fish like that. Some never do. I never have."

"Oh it was such a beautiful fish!"

"It was that, Miss Penelope Royale!"

Whatever happened after that, Nina didn't know.

She was too tired to notice.

CHAPTER THREE: THE ROBBER BARON

The Robinson Mansion—it was of course always written with capital letters—had been built sometime in the nineteen twenties. She could remember her parents talking about it in tones of awe and wonder, which were the tones all mortal and rather ordinary citizens of Bay St. Lucy used to describe it.

Of course, they used the same tones to describe the builder of said mansion, the dark and enigmatic entrepreneur Homer Baron Robinson. Who was grist for the mill of an unending supply of gossipy questions and answers that were equal parts convincing and absurd.

"He's from New Orleans, isn't he?"

"I heard he was originally from Chicago."

"But how did he make his money?"

"Timber."

"Oil."

"Rice."

"Stock deals."

"Land development."

"He's a gangster."

No one offering these answers had the slightest idea about who Homer Baron Robinson actually was, how he made his money, what his politics were, or anything else about him. But that made things all the better, for nothing so inhibits true, pure, effective gossip as a few hard facts. Lacking these, the gossiper experiences the rarified air of unfettered creativity, and becomes something of a cross between Correggio and Shakespeare.

"They say he killed somebody in Memphis, but he got off!"

And voila, *Hamlet*.

"I heard that house he's building cost more than a million dollars."

Monet.

"No, more like five million is what I heard!"

Picasso.

And so on and so on.

All of these rumor threads remained to cover the Bay St. Lucy beaches and streets like cobwebs in an old attic, untouched and sacrosanct, since Homer Baron Robinson proved reclusive, as did his wife. He was seen in the stores, of course; he tipped his hat—he often wore a hat, a white fedora—smiled, and passed the time of day. His wife did the same, except that she did not remove her hat.

Then, in 1964, both of them died.

Apparently while traveling in Europe.

No one knew precisely how they died, at least no one in Bay St. Lucy.

But within a year, Homer Baron Robinson Jr.—a man at least forty years of age—had installed himself in the mansion, along with his wife.

And if the town's residents were shocked at the death of their most shadowy resident, all the more so were they shocked at the appearance of the man's son, who hadn't been known to exist, and his wife. She was slightly more than average height and slightly less than average color, except that she did wear a hat, and didn't have quite her husband's way of bending forward when he spoke, her own habit tending more in the backwards direction, as though the soft, "Good morning," she whispered had a recoil which forced her ever-so-slightly backward.

And then there were the children.

Arthur and Emily.

Ghost children of a haunted house.

Their faces could be seen on occasion peering out of the upstairs windows, gaunt and pale, unsmiling, motionless, gazes fixed either on the vehicles passing along Breakers Boulevard—which the mansion faced—or the ocean—which the mansion ignored, being, in and of itself, also one of the natural elements of the world.

Homer was seven years old when the Robinsons finally moved into their mansion.

Emily was twelve.

They did not go to school.

The rumor was that this was illegal, all children having the legal obligation to go into the cinder block buildings that were Bay St. Lucy's elementary, middle, and high schools, so that they could learn all things leading to second year geometry and algebra, along with the causes of the Peloponnesian War and the poems of William Makepeace Thackeray, and thus be equipped to converse about these things in the barber shops and insurance offices, along with all other citizens of Bay St. Lucy and, later on, the rest of Mississippi.

Which was *not*, of course, (Thank God for Arkansas) the least literate state in the nation.

So people wondered why the Robinson children didn't go to school, and why the Robinson parents were not put in jail for imprisoning them in a haunted mansion.

But no one did anything about it.

As for socializing, very little of that went on. Perhaps one evening of the month, in late summer or early spring, a big black automobile could be seen parked haughtily in the circular driveway, its exhaust pipes pointed threateningly at vehicles passing on the two-hundred-yard distant boulevard.

Perhaps a shadowy figure or two could be seen milling in the gardens, sipping champagne in a white gazebo.

Or perhaps not.

Perhaps that was an illusion.

But illusion or not, Homer Baron Robinson Jr. ran Bay St. Lucy.

If only from the privacy of his study, but he ran it.

The city council took orders from him; and, as Nina had told Frank earlier, even the school board took orders from him.

And all of these things, then, ran through Nina's mind as she and Frank crunched into the white gravel traffic circle with their Volkswagen. A little car such as theirs seemed completely out of place, but there it was.

They got out of the car and waited for a servant to come and tell them what to do.

There was no servant; just light that seemed to sprinkle down like gold dust on the car's roof.

That and the tinkle of recorded music, old and filled with static, hanging in the air but originating nowhere at all.

"What do we do?" whispered Nina.

Frank shook his head:

"The invitation mentioned the garden. It's got to be around in the back of the house."

And so, dutifully, they walked around the corner of the mansion, being careful not to step on freshly watered grass.

The backyard opened before them, willows bending low and brushing the lawn, and acacias exuding both color and aroma. Several white metal tables dotted the area, but only one of them had been set, and only one of them glowed dark yellow, its crystal glasses and silverware sparkling in the sunset.

"Mr. and Mrs. Bannister."

This from a tall, fragile, willowy woman who was walking toward them.

She hadn't risen from the table; she hadn't come around the opposite corner of the house.

She had, Nina found herself thinking, merely appeared a few inches above the ground, like one of the ladies of the night in an old *Dracula* movie.

"I'm Evelyn Robinson. It's such a pleasure to have you over."

"The pleasure is all ours," answered Frank.

Of course, Nina found herself thinking, that was not true. This was not a pleasure, it was an obligation. A business obligation. They did not belong here.

"I hope," the woman said, "that the two of you like oysters?"

Nina, obligatorily:

"We do. We certainly do."

"Wonderful. We were able to get some very fine ones. Come. Join me at the table. My husband is still in his study up on the second floor and offers his regrets. Business matters take up so much of his time. I'm sure he'll be finished shortly, though."

"It's quite all right; I'm sure he has a lot to do," said Frank, who had no idea at all what Homer Baron Robinson Junior did or didn't have to do.

"And I hope white wine will be acceptable?"

Nina:

"Of course."

They reached the table and sat down. For a time useless and insipid small talked spilled across the table until, "It's so gracious for you to have," and, "It's our great pleasure to have," were replaced with a comment made to Nina:

"My husband speaks often of you, my dear."

"I beg your pardon?"

"He says he's heard from numerous sources that you are the most creative teacher in the school, and the most talented."

Nina was shocked.

How did this man even know of her existence?

And why did he care about the school at all, if he was not sending his own children there?

"Well, I'm flattered."

"You should be. And so should you be flattered, Mr. Bannister, about the compliments you have received around town. 'A superb young lawyer!' Homer says about you."

And once again Nina found herself thinking:

How does he know this?

But there was no way to tell.

So let it drop, take the compliments, and eat.

The sun set and the meal progressed.

Between courses—a wedge of lettuce followed, calling itself salade de laitue au Roquefort—Evelyn Robinson said:

"My husband's name, as well as that of his late father, is a bit of an inside joke, and I've urged him at various times to have it changed. You see, Homer Baron is a character from Faulkner's short story, 'A Rose for Emily.' Miss Emily Grierson, a wealthy young woman growing into spinsterhood, becomes enamored with this rakish railroad man who comes to her small town in order to complete a construction project. When she learns that he doesn't intend to do the right thing by her, she poisons him."

"With arsenic," said Nina.

Evelyn Robinson smiled:

"I should have remembered that I was in the presence of a teacher. And a Mississippi one, at that."

"Yes. We know our Faulkner around here."

"So," asked Frank, "what happens after Miss Emily gives her lover the arsenic?"

The woman sitting across the table from Nina blushed ever so slightly. But that was hardly a surprise, for she did everything ever so slightly. She brought ever so slightly her food to her mouth, chewed it ever so slightly after its arrival, swallowed it ever so slightly, digested it ever so slightly and, of course,—though Nina could only speculate as to this last matter—excreted it and disposed of it in the subtlest manner possible.

This was, she decided, a woman who did things not by half but by quarter degrees.

A woman whose entire life was the pale pink color of her bled-dry gown.

"She lets him, well, decay, for the next twenty years. In her bed."

These are, Nina found herself thinking, some weird people.

They did not grow less weird as the back yard darkened, a sliver of moon appeared over the ocean, and one star after another appeared in the balmy, late spring sky.

Still no Homer Baron Robinson.

In his place, though, the two children arrived, carrying dessert: pudding de pain nois aux pecan.

These entities—children as well as pudding—approached soundlessly, so that they were within ten feet of the table before Nina was even aware of them. It was as though each was encased in a kind of translucent bubble, so that the entire atmosphere within which all movements took place had been made antiseptic, pure, and devoid of both life and human interest. Both children had in their eyes the same look Nina had seen in their mother's: a look beyond things near and obvious, a look that seemed fixed on points beyond, the ocean possibly, since there was without question an ocean out there, but another universe more probably, since the sea came and went with tides, and the gaze of the minor Robinson family members—the wife being a minor member also—never changed.

What, Nina found herself thinking, *were they all looking at?*

"Our treasures, ready for bed. Are you both finished with your homework?"

Their gaze still fixed upon that other world.

And the two of them answering simultaneously:

"Yes, Mother."

"Good. And did it pose any difficulties for you?"

"No."

"That is also encouraging to hear. You may both say good night to Mr. and Mrs. Bannister then."

Both children did so.

And then they disappeared.

They did not *run off,* nor did they take an old and accustomed path back into the house, a trail with toys scattered along the way or a secret path pockmarked with hiding places and small cave-like nooks.

No, they simply vanished into the heavy, balmy, and suddenly oppressive early evening air.

And they would not, Nina knew, be seen again until morning.

Five minutes later, another figure appeared, not the enigmatic host whose father had been named for a deceased Faulkner character, but a near-decrepit black man, dressed in a tuxedo, moving from the house across the garden with the speed of an ebb tide.

He approached the table, bent slightly more than he was already bent, and said quietly to Frank:

"Mr. Robinson will see you now, sir."

Frank rose, nodded, and answered:

"I'm ready when he is."

"If you will come this way then."

And the two of them left, Frank following a few steps behind.

He's not even going to come out and introduce himself, thought Nina.

Who are these people?

The sky, despite being dotted with all those stars not obscured by the meek network of lights from downtown Bay St. Lucy, had become unutterably black.

It was a Mississippi night sky, and no one who has not lived in Mississippi knows the blackness of it. Nina had often wondered about the phenomenon.

A lack of industry? The presence of so much agriculture?

The geographical presence of the state on this particular part of the North American continent?

None of those things would seem to explain it. But there were in the universe inexplicable things, and so Nina simply let it go at that.

"Are you happy in your marriage, dear?"

The words originated in Evelyn Robinson, hovered a time over the candle, warmed themselves there, and then made the trip onward and into Nina's perception, where they waited aimlessly for a time, like immigrants at Ellis Island at the turn of the century, not knowing where to go or what to do.

Finally they moved in-country and settled down, planting roots so that they could be perceived, dealt with, and, ultimately, answered:

"Yes. Frank and I are very happy."

There was a slight change in Evelyn Robinson's expression. It slipped quickly from what might be called flat-affect to bemused near-notice and then back to complete uncaring, while somewhere in the process a few words slithered out, like fish swimming into a trap.

"I'm happy to hear it. What else, after all, is there?"

Bowling, Nina thought, but she said nothing, thinking only:

How long am I going to have to sit here with this woman?

As it turned out, she had to sit with the woman almost half an hour. During this time there were comments about how much Evelyn Robinson admired the people of Bay St. Lucy, and how much she yearned to help them in some way. There were comments about her vision of the town, and how wonderful it would be if Bay St. Lucy could become an artists' colony, with gifted people of all races living here together.

And finally:

"It all slips away, doesn't it, Mrs. Bannister? It seems so promising, and then it isn't really at all anymore. Just a façade."

Silence for a time, then:

"One wonders what could have been done. To stop it, I mean. To stop it slipping. Was there one point, I mean, at which an intervention could have been possible? But of course you're young and happy. Ah! I believe your husband is finished. It was delightful having the two of you over tonight."

"The pleasure was all ours," lied Nina, who'd found none of it pleasant.

Frank did, in fact, approach the table.

Homer Baron Robinson never appeared.

Proper good byes were said.

So that, within fewer than ten minutes, Nina and Frank were in their Volkswagen, Breakers Boulevard ribboning out in front of them, the tide coming in to their left, and the town glowing to their right.

There was no silence because of the rumbling of the sea, the grumbling of the four-cylinder engine, and the mumbling of Frank about some useless pleasantries that Nina didn't care to toy with.

But whatever silence there was, she finally pierced by saying, quietly:

"Frank?"

"Yes?"

"I hate you."

"Why?"

"Why not?"

"You have to be more specific than that."

"No I don't. I can hate you if I want, no questions asked."

"Give me a hint."

"All right. You left me out there in the garden alone for thirty minutes."

"Was it that long?"

"By the clock. In my mind it was four years."

"It couldn't have been *that* bad."

"It was worse. You remember her telling us Homer Baron Robinson was named for a Faulkner character poisoned by crazy old Emily Grierson in *A Rose for Emily*?"

"Yes."

"Well, meet Emily."

"Really?"

"There is at most a day between her, him, and the arsenic."

"Well, she's probably been under a lot of stress, moving here to a town where she doesn't know anybody."

"She's a nut."

"You're too judgmental. We're going to be working with the Robinsons."

Silence for a time.

Frank negotiated a turn that led toward the south part of Bay St. Lucy.

The silence continued until it was broken by some gulls screaming and Nina succeeding in not screaming.

But merely asking:

"What?"

Frank glanced her way. "We're going to be working with the Robinsons."

"Will you," she said, quietly, "stop the car so I can go out and lie down in front of it so you can run over me?"

"No."

"Why not?"

"Get the tires all dirty." He grinned. He bumped over some small rocks lining the beach and parked the car. The Gulf of Mexico loomed in front of them, its surface shining in the moonlight. Frank rolled down the car window on his side, letting in the briny-smelling air off the water. Nina rolled down the window on her side and took a deep breath.

"You could buy new ones. And I would be through with it all. Cremated. Finished. Done. No more Evelyn Robinson. It's not a bad deal, really. And after all, how much could new tires cost?"

"You really hate her that much?" Frank reached his hand over and rubbed Nina's neck and shoulders.

"I don't hate her; I'm sorry for her." Nina shrugged her shoulders against his hand.

"Why?"

Nina turned in her seat to face Frank and he dropped his hand. "Frank, do you know what *psychotic* means? Or *manic depressive*? Or *schizoid*?"

"Those are three completely different diseases, Nina."

"Cancer, tuberculosis, and mumps are three different diseases; that doesn't mean you can't have them all at once."

"Evelyn Robinson does not have the mumps."

"You don't know that. And as for the rest, everything that can be wrong with a person's mind is wrong with her mind."

"I thought she was just a typical southern woman with breeding, money, and education."

"You think all intelligent southern women are psychotic?"

"Of course not. Just, like I said, if you'd been listening to me, just the ones with money. And speaking of money..."

"We were speaking of crazy." Nina leaned her head against Frank's shoulder.

"Let's speak of money instead."

Nina sighed. "You never let me finish a thought. Let's get out and walk along the beach."

They did so.

Far offshore, perhaps a mile or so, Nina could see the lights of an offshore drilling rig.

Above, in the soon-to-be summer sky, curled the tail of Scorpio the Scorpion, with bright red Antares twinkling in the center of the beast's thorax.

"Homer Baron Robinson wants to hire me."

At just that moment—nine-fifteen to be exact—the tide finished coming in, looked around, saw nothing truly new or worth sticking around for, and decided to go back out again.

Nina watched as it did all these things, then said:

"What?"

Frank didn't speak at first, and thought about the question, and decided it merited one repetition as an answer:

"Homer Baron Robinson wants to hire me."

"To do what? Have his wife institutionalized?"

"Will you leave her alone?"

A shooting star flashed across the sky directly above them.

It did nothing to help Nina's frame of mind.

"If people leave her alone much longer, Frank, she's going to set fire to the house."

"You don't know that. Besides, it's not our business."

"It wasn't our business. But—and correct me if I'm wrong —if you go into *business* with him, then his wife is our *business*; do you see the point I'm making here?"

"I see, but—"

"Back out," she insisted.

"It's just that—"

"Back out."

"I can't."

"Can too."

"Can't."

"Why not?"

"I gave my word."

"You—"

"I gave my word."

"Frank, what the hell does that have to do with anything? We're talking about *the law* here!"

And the ocean, just to their left, vast and purple dark, seething and swelling and growling and—the ocean frightened and fascinated her simultaneously, as it always had.

"I know. Call me an idealist."

"I'll call you worse than that if I have to talk to Lucretia Borgia again."

"Evelyn Robinson."

"Don't correct me when it comes to psychotics."

Neither of them spoke for a time.

A gull flew low overhead, screeching.

Out of the corner of her left eye she caught a glimpse of a dark shape, perhaps a hundred or so yards out. She saw it break the moon-sparkled surface of the water, hang suspended for a moment, and then disappear beneath a foam-crested swell.

This sight improved her mood a bit, and her tone was softer as she asked:

"So what is this *business* that he wants you involved in?"

"Land development."

"Frank, what do you know about land development?"

"Nothing," he answered.

"Okay, that's a good start."

He put an arm around her, then said:

"But I do know about closings."

"What?"

They were walking just beyond the scarcely perceptible tracing where the last incoming wave lost all impetus in its invasion of the beach and gave up, ready to evaporate and leave beneath it soft dark and lusciously squishy sand that was a joy to walk barefoot on.

Nina almost suggested taking off their shoes, but memories of Evelyn Robinson prevented her from being quite so joyous.

Why did she find the woman so—what, frightening?

"Okay," Frank continued. "Here's the deal: Robinson has control now of about a hundred acres just north of Bay St. Lucy."

"What's north of Bay St. Lucy? Just marshland, isn't it?"

"It is now, but he's had engineering reports. It's going to take massive amounts of land buildups and soil implants, but he can transform that area into housing lots."

"There are some houses out there now, aren't there?" she asked, pulling his arm more tightly around her and scanning the sky for more shooting stars, the sea for more leaping porpoises.

She saw neither.

"Not much more than shacks. He wants to build hundred thousand dollar three- and four-bedroom homes."

"For whom, Frank?"

"Mostly retirees. He's got contacts not only in New Orleans but in Chicago, New York—the man is immensely well connected."

"As opposed to his wife, who has a screw loose."

They'd come almost a mile now from where they'd left the Volkswagen. At that point there were still a few seaside shacks with lamps burning on their stilt-high porches.

But now there was nothing.

Simply water to the left and dune after dune to the right.

Somewhere, far behind her, she could hear the mournful wail of a siren back in Bay St. Lucy.

Her kids. Hers and Frank's, when they came along.

Would they resemble the two faceless automatons she'd encountered tonight?

"Will you forget about that, Nina? Okay, so his family isn't like your family was, or mine. The main thing is, he wants to transform Bay St. Lucy in the right way. He's going to put in a golf course, for heaven sakes!"

"And why once again are all these wealthy people going to come here?"

"Because they're snowbirds. They want to be warm in December, and they want to be able to drive over every day or so and put their feet in the ocean. They'll buy paintings from craft shops."

"We don't have any craft shops."

"We will have. The money these folks bring in is going to turn Bay St. Lucy into an artists' community."

She stopped.

She did not know precisely why.

Perhaps it was the visualization of golf courses in Bay St. Lucy.

Or perhaps it was the memory of all the rumors she'd heard during her youth, and now, about the Robinsons.

Gangsters.

Killers.

Would these be the kind of people Frank was helping to bring here?

Perhaps it was these thoughts that made her stop.

Or perhaps it was just the unutterable loneliness of the unending stretch of dune and beach that loomed before them.

"Frank," she said, "let's go back. We've come far enough."

He nodded.

"Okay."

They turned and began retracing their steps toward the clump of lights that was Bay St. Lucy.

She continued the conversation:

"So he's going to have to foreclose on people who own the land now?"

"Not at all. He's giving them a great price for the patches of land they own now. The truth is, most of them would love to sell. They're getting practically no return on the land—can't fish it, can't farm it—and they've got to pay city taxes."

"And you come in?"

"There will be a huge number of closings—eighty or ninety, all to take place in the next few months. We'll actually reincorporate and become a title company as well as a law firm. There's an immense amount of legal work that goes with this kind of thing."

Nina was silent for a time.

Finally she said:

"I have a bad feeling about this, Frank."

"Why are you so worried? His wife? His kids?"

She shook her head:

"I wish I knew. I just think you should turn him down. You'll do okay without him."

"If I don't take this work, Nina, someone else will. There'll be more attorneys."

The lights of the town were glowing more brightly now, and the tracery line they were following was receding from the land.

"All right. So how much is he going to pay you?"

"It'll be a monthly retainer, and not reckoned by each individual closing."

"And so how much?" she asked, looking up at him and glimpsing another shooting star.

He told her.

"Wow," she said, quietly.

"Yeah. Wow."

"I don't know, I just..."

The shooting star, having neatly bisected Scorpio's tail, disappeared.

"Nina, I've already figured it out in my head. You know that three-story old two bedroom, three houses down from Hope and Paul Reddington's?"

She nodded:

"With the big maple in the back yard?"

"That's the one. Well, the way I figure it—seven months."

"Seven months?"

"If I work with this man for seven months, and he pays me what he's apparently offering—we'll be able to get a loan, and make the down payment on that house."

"So that when Furl comes along…"

"He'll have a great yard to play in. With a privacy fence."

She breathed deeply.

The ocean breathed deeply.

And within a few minutes they were back at their car.

Two hours later she still hadn't gone to bed.

She could think of nothing but the new house Frank and she would buy.

We could paint the living room this way and the dining room this way and we would need a new sofa and there had never been a proper honeymoon and they could take a couple of days and go to the Monteleone and maybe breakfast at Brennan's and…

And like that and like that.

Except at ten thirty, bedtime, Nina had begged off.

She needed to walk.

There were several places Nina went when she needed to walk. One was, of course, the sea shore.

The waves, the sand beneath her feet.

But you couldn't read while walking along the sea shore.

For reading there was the pink granite rock jetty.

There were lights along the jetty.

So she walked out there tonight, all the way to the end, where she could feel the spray of the waves. She had on her yellow slicker, so the water didn't bother her.

She sat down on a drenched boulder that somehow had a flat side up and was above water.

The yellow light glared down at her.

And she took from her immense pocket the small paperback book that she needed tonight.

Goethe. *Faust*.

A deal with the devil.

And caught in the middle of it, young Gretchen. Who'd never done anything wrong in her life.

The last scene. Gretchen, horrified, seeing the smoke seep up from a fissure in the ground and then saying:

"What is that thing that comes up from the ground in this holy place? What does he want? What does he want?"

And then the realization.

She even felt that she could understand the German:

"Er will mich."

He wants me.

CHAPTER FOUR: THE FALL OF ICARUS

The next nine weeks clipped along at a nice pace. No subterranean creature came to get Nina.

The land closings began.

Which meant money.

Nina was astonished at how many details the land development business involved. Of course, owners had to be identified, contacted, dealt with, made happy, and brought in for meetings. Buyers had to be identified, contacted, dealt with, made happy, and brought in for meetings, preferably at the same time as the sellers. Those processes were not too surprising to Nina. What was more surprising was the entire business of platting. The acres north of Bay St. Lucy belonged to the city township, of course, but they also belonged to Wynbottom County. This meant that every plat of land surveyed and reproduced in multiple copies had to go before two boards, each board meeting monthly, yet skewed to bi-weekly schedules. In short, the county might approve Plat 37, given that the specifications for the culvert at the corner of Mandeville and Durbison Roads was increased in size to accommodate the once in a hundred years rain that was supposed to happen, and would, if not for ninety-eight years, then at least sometime.

But the city might not approve, or, more likely, would approve given that something else be done.

All of this took time, phone calls, letters, apologies, subtle yelling into the telephone (never real yelling because this was The South), and a degree of professionalism that Nina had never experienced in Frank, mainly because she'd never seen him so swamped with work.

So this is what a lawyer really did, she found herself thinking.

No last-second hysterical admissions of guilt in a crowded courtroom.

Just road specifications and bridge abutments.

But that was all right.

Because, as the development grew inch by inch and row by row (time to watch St. Lucy's garden grow), the Bannisters' bank account grew along with it.

A nice commission check every two weeks, just as Mr. Robinson had promised.

This led to late afternoon summer car rides through various neighborhoods, paper cups filled with coffee, the sunlight glow slanting through wisteria and magnolia foliage, traffic slow to non-existent, and various houses checked out.

"I love that one. Look at that screened in porch."

"Yeah. It's nice."

"Do you like it better than the one back there on Ross Avenue?"

"Yes. Except for the dormer windows. It doesn't have those."

"How many bedrooms do you think it has?"

"A house that size? Three at least. Maybe four."

"Are we sure we want two stories?"

"I think so. I'm not sure about the yard though."

They asked themselves these kinds of questions with the speed of machine gun fire. It didn't matter who was speaking at any one time. They were, she and Frank, basically one person anyway, just a single being composed of two halves. If one of them hadn't been presupposed to ask about the number of bedrooms, then the other certainly would have.

Always in the back of their minds was the money, the account, the savings, the total sum growing and growing and growing and reaching toward that golden sum which would be a suitable down payment.

"And so, if we gave them their asking price…"

"You never do that."

"Yes but if we did, then the monthly mortgage would be…"

"Would it be that much? We couldn't afford that, could we?"

And on and on and on.

While their little car chugged through the darkening streets of Bay St. Lucy, and the little town went to sleep around them, and the moon grew to its white plum fullness, and the stars dotted the black sky, and the ocean growled and murmured, and their future lives and future family sprouted like a mental, multi-colored tapestry before and between and through and around and in front of and behind and over and under them.

This went on until the middle of August.

School had started on the tenth of August.

This was an ungodly time to be going back, and opening of classes was usually associated with Labor Day, or, at worst, the last day or so of August.

But the previous year had been a terrible one for the run down edifices that constituted the school's physical plant, and burst pipes had forced classes to be cancelled for two weeks in February.

These weeks had to be made up.

And so—

—School in sweltering mid-August.

But Nina was taking it okay.

Until, at 2:43 on a Wednesday afternoon—she was always surprised, later on in life, when she recounted various events, she found she could remember the time so precisely—her sixth period class was interrupted. As a young teacher, she'd been learning steadily. The eight o'clock literature class was either too sleepy or too hyper—depending on the personality type of the student—to be cognizant of much that was going on, and the fifty minutes during which she had charge of them served mostly to be sure they'd put their clothing on correctly and remembered where their lockers were. Second period, nine to nine-fifty, was clearly the best time of the day. "The moon was a ghostly galleon, tossed on cloudy seas," "The highwayman came riding," and any number of scenes from "The Sea Wolf," actually reached a few of the students and made their eyes sparkle with imagination and not glaze from mental inertia.

Ten to ten-fifty saw a few more such signs of hope, making her wonder if at least a few of the freshman class she taught third period might become little Nina Bannisters, that is, people who lived most of their lives in literature and gave only the slightest lip service at all to what was optimistically called reality.

Eleven to one was lunch. If not actually eating it, then preparing for it, going to it, playing with it, putting it away, and beginning the process (around one o'clock usually) of digesting it.

The rest of the day was maximum security prison, inmates praying for the three o'clock bell and access to their or their boyfriends' cars.

It was at this moment of near bliss, air hanging heavily in the colorless classroom, books all piled neatly where they belonged, the wall clock moving with torturous and morbid dalliance, when a knock came at the door.

Six students jumped to their feet, all desperate to do something that might get them to the edge of the room, if not actually outside of it.

"Jason. Get the door."

"Yes, ma'am!" exulted Jason.

The other five, lost in lost hope, still continued to stand.

"Thomas, Sidney, Mary, George, Peter—sit down."

"Can we…"

"No."

"Can I…"

"No. Sit down."

They did so.

Jason, a Greek hero now in search of the Argo and the Golden Fleece, strode manfully, freed for some seconds of the straight jacket that was his desk, to the door.

And opened it.

There, dressed like an upright crow in all black, stood Principal Adelia Wickersley.

What have I done now? thought Nina.

Morning attendance? Lunch money? Week's lesson plans?

No, she made sure that.

And then she looked into the face of Mrs. Wickersley and she knew.

This was none of those things.

"Mrs. Bannister?"

"Yes?"

"Can you come outside for a second, into the hall?"

All of the students were looking at her.

None of them were sleeping.

Their eyes were wide.

They were not breathing.

They might have been young, but they were not stupid.

"Continue with what you were doing," said Nina, quietly.

She then walked to the door and outside into the hallway.

It was deserted except for the few coaches who always seemed to be prowling around looking for stray students, remembering in actuality when they were once stray students themselves.

Twenty paces down the hall was the door to the library.

The principal gestured toward it, saying:

"We've cleared the library. Let's go in there."

Nina, now moving almost automatically, heard her own shoes clacking as she made her way along.

She did not speak, nor did Adelia Wickersley.

"In here, Nina."

"All right."

The door to the library was open; she peered inside.

Both librarians were gone; the books stared at her.

Standing by the circulation desk were three police officers. An older ruddy-faced man, a woman of the same age and ruddiness, and the young patrolman she recognized as Moon Rivard.

The three of them joined the books in staring back at her.

"What is it?" said a voice from inside her.

The older man spoke:

"There's been—"

The would-be sentence stopped, as though standing at the edge of a precipice and staring out into space.

Nina did nothing; said nothing; felt nothing.

Moon Rivard:

"Maybe you oughta come and sit down, Mrs. Bannister."

She did so, feeling, as she followed orders, that she herself was walking out over the precipice before which the ominous words had halted, and that, once seated, she would actually be falling in space.

But finally the obligatory actions had taken place, and they all found themselves seated in blue plastic chairs, a library table between them.

The woman:

How did they decide who was to speak?

"There has been an accident, Ms. Bannister."

"Involving whom?"

Nina, always the English teacher.

The objective mood in the face of tragedy.

Because she knew it was tragedy.

And of course, it was.

"You have a student, Penelope Royale?"

"I do. But she's in class. Right now, she's in my fifth period class. Home room. She was in one of my second period classes this morning. I've watched her all day. She couldn't have…"

"Her mother is dead."

Outside, things were happening. The busses had begun to pull up to the curb. A few sixth-period classes had dismissed early. Students were already getting into cars and getting out of cars, and the fringes of the town had begun, for reasons probably unknown to anyone, to mix with the fringes of the high school. The same fringes interacted with Nina's mind, which, never quite at ease, kept spying books on the library shelves, and mentally pulling them out, and mentally opening them, and mentally seeing:

About suffering they were never wrong, The old Masters: how well they understood its human position: how it takes place while someone else is eating or opening a window or just walking dully along.

And there, walking dully along, were two football players in uniform, heading over to the stadium for practice.

They did not understand the story of Icarus and how he'd fallen from the sky.

"How," she heard herself asking, "can she be dead?"

General silence.

"I know she travels for a living. She has to drive a lot. Was there an accident or…"

Moon Rivard turned his blue plastic chair slightly, so that he was facing her, and somehow Nina knew that in the future, throughout her life in Bay St. Lucy, when she and Frank needed to know something, be it good or bad, Moon Rivard would always be the one to tell them.

"Miss Nina—"

"Yes?"

"She did travel some."

"I know! She worked for a cosmetics firm!"

"No, ma'am, she didn't. She didn't work for no cosmetics firm."

Nina stared at him, but the words kept leaping off the shelves and into her brain:

In Breugel's Icarus, for example, how everything turns away quite leisurely from the disaster. The sun shone as it had to…

And, yes, it was true. There was that dreadful golden sunlight spreading itself across the parking lot. Just as it had to—

"I don't understand what you're saying."

And, of course, it had to be Adelia Wickersley, the crow, the shriveled, who said, who was the only one in the room who could have said:

"Penelope's mother was a prostitute."

At that moment the bell rang.

The hall filled with students and noise.

"She was what?"

"A prostitute, Mrs. Bannister. She worked primarily in New Orleans."

The sun shone.

As it had to on the white legs disappearing into the green water, and the expensive delicate ship that must have seen

Something amazing, a boy falling out of the sky,

Had somewhere to get to and sailed calmly on

Penelope's mother had fallen out of the sky.

And now, all of these people in the hallway had somewhere to get to and sailed calmly on.

"How did she die?"

Moon Rivard:

(Thankfully, because Nina did not want to hear this from her principal).

"Dey found her in a room in the Quarter. It was, dey think maybe, the room she used to—"

"I understand. Did one of her customers kill her?"

"No. She died of a drug overdose, so it seem like. She had a drug habit, cost a lot of money. It made her have to work that much the more. We figure dat when she started she could spend a couple of days in New Orleans and then come back and be with her daughter for a week or so. But when the habit got to be worse—"

"I understand."

"So now we have to—"

"I know what we have to do."

"If you want, we can—"

"No. I have to see Penelope before she leaves class."

The policewoman:

"Mrs. Bannister, we have grief counselors."

"I know," said Nina, rising. I'm one of them."

Penelope had not left the classroom. In general, Nina had noted, the young woman tended to avoid crowds. This might have been because of her bulk and strength, and the fact that she tended to take up more space than normal, to bully smaller people without wishing to do so. But on this day it was because of another reason, this being that she was still reading. She sat in a corner, seemingly oblivious to the fact that the bell had rung, her back bent, her eyes hovering low over the red imitation leather volume below her on the desk. Nina recognized the book, and would even have remembered some of the blue ball point pen underlinings that she herself had made in it some years before during her sophomore—sophomore? No, junior—year.

Robert Louis Stevenson's *Treasure Island.*

And how far along are you, Penn?

Have they reached the island yet?

Behind Penelope, and through the wall of glass windows, the world teemed with an entire high school now freed from its stucco brick prison walls, thousands of volts of estrogen and testosterone surging through each other, spilling out onto the sidewalks and flooding the engines of pickup trucks and small Ford cars with distinctive tail fins.

Nina simply stood in the door for some seconds, awaiting the inevitable words that were destined to come out of her mouth, still recalling Jim Hawkins and W. H. Auden, all mixed together:

"Aaaarrrrh, Jim Awwwkins!"

And:

"the sun shone

As it had to on the white legs disappearing into the green

Water, and the expensive delicate ship that must have seen

Something amazing, a boy falling out of the sky,

Had somewhere to get to and sailed calmly on.

There they all went, sailing/driving calmly—well, not so calmly because they were males and females and sixteen years old—on.

"Penn?"

The girl looked up, then behind her.

It seemed to take a second or so for her to realize what reality she was in.

"Oh. I'm sorry. I didn't hear the bell."

"I know."

"I'll just get my stuff out of the desk and—"

"I need to talk to you, Penn."

Penelope stared back for a time, recognizing the tone. Then she asked:

"What did I do?"

"Nothing."

"I've been in class all day. I was home all last night cleaning the place up and doing my homework. I didn't—"

"You didn't do anything, Penn."

"Then what—"

"You just need to come with me."

"Where?"

"We're going out to the jetty."

"But I still don't—"

"Just get your books together and leave them in your locker. You know my car, don't you?"

"Yes, ma'am."

"It's in the faculty parking lot. Put your things together and meet me there."

"All right."

And don't talk to anybody, said Nina to herself.

Especially not the police

No one in Bay St. Lucy knew the age of the jetty, or when it had been built, or by whom. It was simply there, an elemental fact of life, immovable, a half mile long slab of gray spray-soaked concrete buttressed by huge red granite boulders, through whose jagged cracks could be seen crab-infested pools of seawater that surged and ebbed along with the waves and tides.

Some said the town had been built because the jetty was there, and others said the reverse. But it hardly mattered. The jetty was immovable and eternal, the town a wisp of hope that had never been very certain and from day to day wavered on extinction. Bay St. Lucy was not much. It was not a thriving fishing village, nor a chic tourist spot, nor a hub of intercostal maritime activity. Its high school teams neither won nor competed in state championship finals. It was there because the parents of its inhabitants had always been there, and could conceive of going nowhere else, of living nowhere else. It had room for two grocery stores, two insurance companies, one auto mechanic, one drug store—and it had room for, Nina fervently hoped, two lawyers.

But that did not matter. Whatever happened to it, there was the jetty.

The jetty was a place for being alone, and it was for that purpose Nina had always used it. When her parents died of cancer within two months of each other, she'd come here. She found no answers in the mist and scudding clouds and growling waves, but she did find a surcease in the need to ask questions.

She had come here after the first kiss from Frank.

And after Frank's proposal, when the waves—green waves that day—had been laughing and the porpoises leaping with joy, smiles unmistakably beaming from their gray black glistening submarine fuselage bodies.

And now she was here with Penelope, sitting on the very end of the spray-slicked slab, both of them in canvas shoes which had slipped repeatedly on their walk out from the beach.

Penelope, during this walk, had seemed as elemental as the jetty itself, and her body could have been one of the mass boulders, had it been stripped of clothing and covered with salt-froth and foam.

For the depths—

Who had written that?

Well, it didn't matter.

Whoever had written it wouldn't have bothered much about proper documentation.

For the depths, of what use is language?

And these were the depths.

"Penelope, there's something I have to tell you."

The two were sitting side by side, feet just above the water, the new God's fingernail moon just rising—red sky at night, sailor's delight—hanging by an invisible thread about Cuba or Puerto Rico or Western Florida or whatever part of the world lay just beyond that line of water-horizon.

"It's Mom, isn't it?"

"Yes."

"Is she dead?"

"Yes."

Silence.

Though not silence, of course, never silence, thank God no silence because the ocean would not allow it. No horrible, unthinkable, whiteness of the whale, either, because that whiteness meant absolute nothingness and the ocean meant eternal something, green or blue or white or whatever God chose for it to be at that time…

…but something.

So it filled what would have been silence with its scudding and roaring.

"They just came and told me, Penn. Apparently she died of—"

"I know how she died."

"You know?"

"Yes. I know I do dumb things, but I'm not stupid."

"No. I know that."

"After Dad left us, she really did work on the road. Selling cosmetics, I mean."

"Yes."

"I don't know how she started with the—with the things she was taking. There was never enough money."

"You don't know where your dad is?"

"No. No idea. But it was me."

"What was?"

"The problem. She wanted to take care of me. Get me all the right things, you know."

"She loved you."

"But I was the cause of it."

"You can't say that."

"She would have made it on her own all right. But having to take care of me, get me clothes, be sure I was at school on time, all that—it was just too much for her. So somehow to hold it together in her mind, she started on the—other things. And then she had to buy them. She needed more money, and selling cosmetics wasn't enough. She had to sell—whatever else she had."

"I understand."

"I did, too. When she wasn't there at night, I understood. Like I say, I'm not stupid. I saw her in the morning when we were getting ready, taking showers, all that. I saw the marks on her arm. I remember thinking they were like a train track that just kept getting longer. With the train, whenever it came, just going straight into her arm."

A flight of seagulls screeched overhead.

One of the red-purple clouds obscured, then revealed, the white bright sliver of moon.

"So it was my fault."

"No it wasn't, Penn. None of it was your fault."

"Where was she?"

"A place in New Orleans. In the Quarter."

"Do they know how much she must have suffered?"

"They didn't tell me."

"From what I can understand, it isn't that bad. You just go to sleep."

"I'm sure that's the way it was."

"That wouldn't be so bad, you know? Just going to sleep? I think about that some time."

"Don't."

"You have to think about something. Sometimes there's nothing else to think about."

"There's always something else to think about."

"Yeah. Like what's going to happen to me."

"That won't be a problem."

"No. I'll go to a home."

"Yes. But it'll be a real home. It won't be a foster home, or an institute of some kind."

"How can you say that? Who's going to want me?"

"We will, Penn. Frank and I."

"You two would want me in your house?"

"Of course. And we're not the only ones. You won't be sent away."

"I don't know. I just—"

She put her hands to her face. Nina could see tears seeping through her tightly clinched fingers.

There was nothing to say, so the two of them simply sat for a time listening to the waves, the gulls, and Penelope's sobbing.

Finally another sound interposed itself, this one coming from the beach. Nina turned and saw, at the base of the jetty, a growing caravan of colors and movement. A crowd had amassed, as well as several vehicles, at least two of which were police cars with blue and red lights flashing.

Penelope saw it too.

It took her a time to dry her eyes and get her voice under control.

"What's happening now?" she asked.

Nina shook her head.

"I don't know. I think Bay St. Lucy is happening."

"Are they coming to take me to jail? Do they think I did something?"

"They're not coming to take you to jail. They're coming to help you. It's your town, Penn."

"Look at them. There must be fifty people down there."

"There will be more."

"I don't think I can take being around anyone just now. Go and tell them to leave. I just want to stay out here. I want to be out on the ocean with this water around me, and these rocks. I can't take people right now. I think about what's going to happen to me. And then, to stop that, I try to think about something else. But that something else turns into what it must have been like for mom, in those last hours, when she was alone in that room—"

Nina said nothing, but thought:

'The mind is its own place, and of itself can make a hell of heaven, or a heaven of hell.'

Oh John Milton, where are you when we need you?

Right here, as it seems.

"We have to go now."

Penelope nodded.

"I know."

"There are a lot of things that have to get done."

"I know that, too."

"None of them will be fun. But you have to realize, you're not alone."

"I think, maybe, everybody is alone."

"Only if we want to be. And you can't want to be. So let's go, okay?"

"Okay."

And they did.

The scene on the shore was pandemonium, with doctors, nurses, housewives, police officers, and first aid providers all waiting for them as they reached the end of the jetty. Penelope was engulfed by a throng of women, all with tears in their eyes, all saying things like, "You dear girl!" and, "It'll be all right!" and, "You've got to eat something!"

Chicken salad.

At least two of the women would have brought chicken salad.

Sherwood Anderson had written, *For the depths, of what use is language?*

Bay St. Lucy's version of that was: *For the depths, there must be chicken salad.*

But just as Penelope had been engulfed by the women of the town, with the town's police and first aid units standing on their perimeter, so Nina was engulfed by Frank, who held her hand tightly and slipped an arm around her waist.

"Nobody knew where you two had gone!"

She put her head against his chest; now she was crying.

"You should have known. You should have known where I always go. The jetty."

"I did know. But it took them a while to find me. In the meantime everybody was worried that the girl might have committed...well, I don't know, that she might have—"

"I know what you mean. And I guess she might have done something like that. But we needed to talk first. I needed to be with her."

"If you had just told somebody—"

"They wouldn't have let us alone."

"Damn right they wouldn't."

"How did you find out, Frank?"

"Moon Rivard came by the office about an hour ago. I've been on the phone ever since then, either trying to get in touch with you—I thought you might have taken her home—or finding out whatever I could from the New Orleans police force. After a while I kicked myself and said: 'The jetty. Of course, they're gone to the jetty, that's where Nina always goes when things like this happen."

"Except things like this don't happen. Not things this bad."

"No. Maybe not. Where's the Volkswagen?"

"Over there, parked behind some dunes, so nobody would see it."

"Come on then. We need to talk. All hell is breaking loose."

Within two minutes they were seated in the car, Frank behind the wheel and Nina in the passenger seat.

Frank started the engine and backed the car up, then pulled forward, slowly.

"Where are we going?" asked Nina.

"Let's go to Gerard Park. Penelope will be okay here; there are at least half a dozen people taking care of her. And Gerard Park is to me what the jetty is to you. It's where I need to go to walk and think."

"All right."

They moved out through the dunes and onto Jackson Avenue, then turned toward the center of town. They passed a yard here, a porch there, a pack of mongrel dogs, and the normal flotsam and jetsam that was Bay St. Lucy in the late afternoon, sunlight lying like a golden blanket over the town.

"So what have you been able to find out, Frank?"

He downshifted and shook his head:

"Not much that you don't already know. It happened in a cheap motel room in The Quarter. One of the maids had come in to clean the room about ten. She called the police. Penelope's mother's ID was in her purse. The address was Bay St. Lucy, and so they called the police office here. All of this took until early afternoon. A group got together and came out to the school, which was just getting out. It took some time to gather the right people to be there when the news was broken to Penelope. Kids react in different ways when they hear terrible things like this. There was a woman psychologist who works for the police. The emergency room was called, just in case some kinds of medication might have been needed. The consensus of all of them was, I think, the best thing was for you to abduct the girl from school and take her half a mile into the ocean where the two of you could go crabbing."

"Come on, Frank."

"Okay, I'm sorry."

They were crawling slowly by the gray granite courthouse now, and she could hear the big circular clock that told time for the downtown businessmen as it tolled five o'clock.

"No, you're probably right. It's just that I'm about the only one Penelope has been able to talk to for a time now."

"Yeah, I know. In retrospect, maybe you did the right thing. They'll probably put you away for a couple of years for kidnapping, and after you get out we'll have a laugh about the whole thing."

"Right. So, what's happening now?"

"About a million things have to happen, all of them traumatic. I'll tell you about them once we get to the park."

It took them no more than two minutes to do so, since Gerard Park sat just to the west of downtown. It was Bay St. Lucy's oldest park, and Nina could understand Frank's love of it. She had played there as a child on the see saws and swings that had been erected years earlier in a far corner, over by the red bandstand.

It was almost deserted now, except for three children who were playing with a scruffy looking collie dog.

Frank parked behind a grove of willow trees.

As they got out of the car, Nina felt a wave of aromas wash over her: acacia trees, myrtles, dogwoods, and all that spring and southern Mississippi could produce by working in tandem.

They began to walk toward the tall white central gazebo.

"Now she asked, "About these million things that are about to happen."

"Well, the first thing, of course, is what to do with Penelope."

"I thought she'd spend the night with us."

"That's a possibility, but several other families have volunteered to take her in."

"For just tonight, or—"

He shook his head:

"Well, that's a problem, of course. No one's sure about what will happen to her, long term."

"She can't be put in a home, Frank. That would kill her."

"I know. But it's a complicated situation. She's an orphan now. How old is she?"

The collie dog and the children chasing after it were now bounding around the gazebo, dog barking happily, children screaming, squirrels in a nearby magnolia bush chattering taunts at the whole group.

"Sixteen I think." Nina pushed back a lock of her hair from her face.

"The possibility of a foster home has to be considered."

"No!"

He pursed his lips.

"That's easy for you to say, Nina."

"Nothing is easy about this."

"No, that's true. But the simple truth is this: having Penelope stay with us tonight, or at the Reddington's tomorrow night—"

"They've volunteered?"

"Just about everybody in town has volunteered."

"Good ole Bay St. Lucy."

They had reached the gazebo now, and were climbing the two steps that led up into it. Nina automatically remembered the small Sunday afternoon picnics that she and her parents had eaten here, usually on a Saturday afternoon, all of them seated on the bench that extended around the cupola, pieces of her mother's fried chicken falling on the gazebo's wooden floor as they ate ravenously.

She and Frank sat down on that same bench, watching as a flock of seagulls flew low over a jungle gym perhaps fifty yards distant.

"Yes, we take care of our own. The problem is, it's one thing to have her stay just for a few nights in someone's house, just as a stopgap measure. To have her live permanently with a family here is something completely different."

"Would she have to be adopted, officially?"

"No. That would be an option, of course. Easier would be to have the court set up a temporary guardianship. But even that isn't as simple as it might seem. The family involved would have to take complete responsibility for Penelope's business matters. Then there are the affairs of her mother to consider."

A young couple appeared, as if by magic, produced somehow by one of the low arching, thickly-leaved and white-blossomed magnolia trees. They appeared to be teenagers, looking like all teenagers look when they are in love and it's summer and they're holding hands and they have a transistor radio with them.

The sounds of the dog and the children and the squirrel and the few slow-passing cars were now somewhat obscured by The Beach Boys, who wished they all could be California Girls.

"What affairs?"

"We don't know, Nina. We don't know her financial situation. She may have, probably does have, debts."

"But she's dead!"

"Death unfortunately does not eliminate debt." A breath of ocean air blew through the open windows of the car.

"God I hate being married to a lawyer."

"That's why I never told you I was one, at least until after we'd had sex together. Then you were hooked."

"Somehow I don't feel like laughing right now."

"I know. Come on, let's go over to the track and walk around it. We're too close to The Beach Boys here."

They rose and made their way across the gazebo, feeling the old floorboards creak beneath their feet as they went.

The long grass they stepped down into was deliciously dew-covered, as though it were early morning and not late afternoon.

Nina took Frank's hand as they moved off toward the running track that lay in the absolute center of the park.

"Go on, Frank. Tell me everything. Somehow I've got the feeling that you're just getting started. There are more problems, I assume."

"There are *only* problems."

"Get at them."

"The house."

"What about it?"

"Well, in the first place it's got Penelope's stuff in it. Her clothes, personal belongings—"

"I understand."

"Someone needs to go to the house, with her, and pack a bag for a few nights."

"I can do that."

"I know, but you may be busy doing other things. You can't be responsible for this whole thing. But at any rate, that's only part of the problem as far as the house is concerned."

"The rest being?"

"I was able to find out some information from the County Clerk's office. Penelope's mother is renting that house."

"From?"

"A company in Vicksburg."

They stepped onto the running track, hearing and feeling red finely-cut cinder particles scratch beneath their shoes as they walked.

"Damn," said Frank, quietly.

"What?"

"Those teenagers. The ones we were trying to get away from. They've followed us over here."

"What's wrong with teen age love?"

"Nothing. It's the Beach Boys I was trying to get away from."

"Just ignore it."

"I'll try."

"Now go on. You were talking about the house. It doesn't seem too much of a difficulty to me. The company can just rent it to somebody else. Problem solved."

"Except that the Royales were three months behind on rent."

"Damn."

The sun had begun to set now. It was half of an orange lying just beyond a row of houses that fronted the park.

Long shadows now covered the infield of the running track.

The Beach Boys were still blaring, still upset about the home states of all those women not born in California.

"Someone's going to have to pay that back rent."

"It can't just be written off?"

"Money can never just be *written off*. Characters in books can be *written off*. But money is real, and it has to come from somewhere, and it has to go somewhere. In this case, the company in Vicksburg may ask that Bay St. Lucy declare Penelope a Ward of The State. In which case, the city would assume responsibility for her debts."

"Okay, so I know that house. It's a little place, not very well kept up. How much could three months' back rent be?"

"I know exactly how much it might be. Seven hundred and fifty dollars—two fifty a month."

"County Clerk's Office?"

"The same."

They had now reached the beginning of the long straightaway that formed the northern side of the oval track.

A white faded chalk line showed them where they were to start running.

Their shoes continued to scrape, scrape, and their steps produced small red clouds from the red cinders beneath them.

"Well, that's not a huge amount of money."

"No, it's not as much as eleven hundred dollars."

"You're not going to make me cuss again, are you?"

"That's up to you."

"So what's eleven hundred dollars?"

"That's the amount that Ms. Royale owed in missed monthly payments on her Oldsmobile."

Nina thought for a time, then said:

"I think I'm ready to go home. Let's head for the car. The park isn't really comforting me."

"No. Me neither."

They cut across the infield of the track, then headed toward the gazebo.

The teenagers, maddeningly, followed them.

She could feel Frank's hand tighten.

"It's all right, Frank."

"Do they think we're their parents?."

"No. If they thought that, then they'd be going the other way. But just—sum up here. How bad does all this get, ultimately?"

He shrugged.

"We don't know. Nobody knows right now. About half an hour ago or so, just before I left to come down here, the mayor called and asked if I'd agree to handle this matter. I said I'd do what I could. He said as far as fees were concerned, the city would try to take care of that."

"And you said we'd do it for free."

"Of course, I did."

"Thank you, Frank."

She put her arm around him as they came within sight of their car.

He shook his head and continued:

"The only problem is, I don't know or have any idea how much of *it* there is. The woman's affairs are in a complete mess, obviously. And finally—well, not finally, because we're not even close to a *finally* on any of this—but *next* is the matter of the funeral."

"Yes. I was trying to avoid thinking of that."

"Somebody's got to think of it."

"Where is the body now?"

They had reached the Volkswagen now. She opened her door and slid into the seat, hearing Frank on the other side of the cab say:

"At the Police Morgue in New Orleans."

Nina shivered. She felt icy fingers running down her back.

"The *Police* Morgue?"

"Yes."

"Why?"

"In cases of drug overdoses there must always be an autopsy, and it must be carried out by the county coroner working in conjunction with the local Police Forensics Group."

"So the body…"

"Will get here when it gets here."

They were silent for a time.

Finally Frank started the engine.

He floored the accelerator.

"Why are you flooring it?" she asked.

"So I can't hear those damned Beach Boys."

They sat for a time until the teenagers were gone, subsumed into the same grove that had produced them.

Then Frank let up on the accelerator, put the car in gear, and began the drive back home.

CHAPTER FIVE: ANOTHER COUNTRY HEARD
FROM

Things proceeded apace.

Not easy things, but the chores and events and meetings and arguments and agreements then disagreements and tears and wan smiles and shakes of the head that make life muddle-through-again even in the midst of its contrary, which of course is death.

First—

Penelope was taken home from the jetty, accompanied by a cadre of well-wishing women who helped her go through the house, find whatever things she needed for a few days' stay elsewhere, and in general keep busy enough doing whatever so that she wouldn't go insane or fill her mind with horrible thoughts about the past, the present, or the future.

Next, the house was cleaned, dishes washed and put away, windows closed and locked, rental company contacted, and invisible signs put on all the walls and all the furniture saying:

A DEAD PERSON USED TO LIVE HERE—RENT ME NOW!

Then Penelope was taken to the Bay St. Lucy Hospital—something Nina found grotesque, useless, and cruel—so that she could be evaluated.

This was done by helpful and professional care givers and grief counselors, all of whom asked different questions, all of those questions boiling down to the same one:

"If we don't medicate you and keep you here, are you going to kill yourself?"

But Penelope was strong, at least on the exterior. The rippling muscles and stern demeanor belied what must have been going on inside her, which Nina could only guess at. But all questions she answered with a quiet determination, a sense of rationality, and the calm assurance that, yes, she might be grieving, but, no, she was not crazy.

She knew that several families had invited her to their houses for as many days as might be needed.

And everything was going to be all right.

There were any number of possibilities for her in the future.

And everything was going to be all right.

She could choose where she wanted to stay tonight; it was simply important that she not be alone, that she take some exercise and eat something nourishing, and, above all, force herself to sleep a little.

And everything was going to be all right.

Which was, of course, not true.

As for Nina, she went home, aware that she was probably taking the whole thing worse than anyone else in Bay St. Lucy, including Penelope.

How could anyone do something like Mrs. Royale had done? Become addicted to a poisonous substance, which could only be purchased by selling one's own body?

She thought of her own wonderful childhood, and she thought of Frank, and how there had never been anyone other than Frank and never would be.

And about how lucky she was.

While she thought of these things she paced along the beach, looking in vain for her two porpoises, which were not there.

Wrong time of day.

She continued to walk until five o'clock, when both Frank and Penelope arrived, he from his office, she from the hospital.

And somehow the three of them got through the night.

They ate something that she cooked, but she didn't remember what it was. They watched something on television, but she didn't remember what it was. They answered the telephone, which rang incessantly; they answered the doorbell, which rang incessantly; they took the plates of food that were offered to them, some of them not even being chicken salad (deviled eggs took second place); they took the Volkswagen down to the beach at nine, watched a sky full of stars, wondered, as the newly grieving always do, if the dead watch down from heaven and, if so, where in heaven, which star exactly; and walked.

Even as they did so, Nina could see Penn's gaze fixed as much on the ocean as on the night sky.

She wants to be out there.

Hopefully she wants to be on the water and not in it.

Then they returned home to find cards that had been stuck in the door and pushed under the door.

Someone had also left a big red metal pot of shrimp gumbo on the entrance porch.

They laughed about this. They had no idea why they laughed; there was simply something funny about shrimp gumbo.

At eleven o'clock it was decided that all should go to bed, Penelope in the spare bedroom, which Nina, being Nina, always kept in a pristine state of cleanliness, as though, Frank was in the habit of joking, the Pope was going to stay there for several nights.

The walls of the room were, of course, covered with books. Nina took out several—*Treasure Island* among them—but decided on another that Penn was to read.

"Look upon this as an assignment."

"An assignment?"

"Yes. You have to go to school tomorrow, you know."

"I know."

"Things have to go on. Like normal, even though we all know they aren't normal."

"Yes."

"So I'm going to assign you to read this book tonight. I don't want you lying in bed and thinking awful thoughts. This isn't too long a book, maybe ninety pages or so. Tomorrow in fifth period class I'm going to test you on it. Now, here, take it. You should finish it about one in the morning."

"What is it?"

"Just take it."

Nina left the book and went to bed.

She and Frank whispered, so that there were no sounds in their little house except the barking of a dog some three hundred yards distant; the ever present growling of a tide coming in down at the beach; and the comings and goings of meteors which made their way gleefully through the belt of Perseus.

"The autopsy, Frank?"

"Maybe tomorrow, maybe the next day."

"What's keeping them?"

Nina couldn't stop thinking of the horrible images connected with the word.

Autopsy.

She had no idea what an actual autopsy consisted of but—

—no that was not quite true.

She did have an idea what an autopsy consisted of.

And that's what made the whole thing so terrible.

"It's New Orleans."

"Why couldn't the autopsy be done here?"

"We're Mississippi; the death occurred in Louisiana."

"All right. But when it's done…"

"They'll fly the body back."

"To?"

"Waynewright Funeral Home."

"Who made those arrangements?"

"I did. I and Tom Waynewright, this afternoon."

Frank was seated on the couch, and she on the big overstuffed green chair beneath the window. That was the normal way they passed evenings, both reading.

But they were not reading now, and she'd begun to feel very much alone.

So she went over and sat close by him on the couch, taking his left arm and looping it around her shoulders.

"When will the funeral be?"

"Probably this weekend."

"Where?"

"First Methodist."

She could see through the window now. A pickup truck passed slowly in front of their house, then turned on Avenue B, making its way toward downtown, where lights had begun to go off.

"She wasn't really a member."

"Yes she was; she just didn't know it."

"Who pays?"

She inched closer to him. It was a hot night, but the warmth she needed—and got—from him had nothing to do with temperature.

"It will get figured out."

"And as for what's going to happen to Penn?"

She could hear him breathing heavily:

"Town meeting tomorrow night."

"Does it have to be so fast?"

"Yes. She needs to know what's going to happen to her. For the next few days, then longer. I'm not saying a final decision has to be made, but *a* decision has to be made, and one that will last for more than just the next few days. Anyway, all the families volunteering to keep her for a while will be there. The city council, Judge Davis. Also, we've invited representatives from two foster homes."

"That would kill her!" said Nina, drawing back a bit, and remembering Penn's words on the jetty.

Frank shook his head:

"No, it wouldn't. It wouldn't kill her. It would take some adjusting. But it wouldn't kill her."

She sighed, then let herself slip back closer to him.

"You don't think she'll have to be sent away, Frank, do you?"

"I think all options need to be explored."

They were silent for a time.

Finally, Nina asked:

"We're going to volunteer to be her guardian, aren't we?"

"Of course. I already did that, this afternoon."

"How?"

"I called Judge Davis."

"And he said?"

"Two other families have also volunteered. We'll just have to wait and see what the meeting brings tomorrow night. Maybe there won't even be a final decision; but the process needs to start."

"All right; I understand."

"We need to go to sleep, Nina."

"Yes. You're right."

And so, of course, she didn't, but she lay in bed when Frank did. He drifted off quickly, but she merely lay quite still, looking up at the ceiling, which she could make out only slightly, imagining that several million miles above it was heaven, which she couldn't make out at all.

At a little after one in the morning, she slipped out of bed, catlike, and crept into the guest bedroom.

Penelope was fast asleep, breathing heavily.

The reading light was still on.

In its glow, Nina could see the cover of the closed novel, which the girl had obviously completed:

Robert Louis Stevenson.

Kidnapped.

The Bay St. Lucy Town Council met in a room directly adjacent to the Bay St. Lucy Jail, which was located directly adjacent to the Bay St. Lucy Courtroom, which was directly adjacent to the offices of the Public Utilities Division, (water and gas) and the Center for Animal Control (dog catcher).

All of these rooms were housed in a flat white building which, with a couple of insurance offices, the law firm competing with Frank's, a small park, and several bait and tackle shops, comprised the town's downtown area.

"I think we need to call the meeting to order."

Judge Richard Davis looked, Nina found herself thinking, exactly as he should have looked: stately, black-suited, dark blue-tied, silver-haired, thoughtful, and fair.

The truth of the matter was, everyone in the room looked exactly as they should have looked, thoughtful and fair, even though the women were not stately and black-suited and the men sported a great variation of tie colors.

It was Penelope that looked out of place.

For, of course, she was out of place.

She wore a black dress, for mourning.

Nina had never seen her in any outfit other than jeans and a baggy sweater, but the effect of the dress she'd been advised—actually, probably, ordered by the court—to wear, was stunning.

Her muscles, usually covered by denim and sackcloth, threated to burst out of the garment which was obviously too small for her, as all garments probably would be, had they not been expressly tailored for a Russian shot-putter.

No, she looked out of place.

But all the others—the families, the Reddingtons— and the Richardsons—these people represented the Great Heart of Bay St. Lucy, and made Nina proud of her little village.

Even the foster home people seemed less menacing than Nina had expected.

"We have all," the Judge continued, "experienced a tragedy. "We heard church bells tolling all over town. And it is, of course, exactly as the poet says: 'Ask not for whom the bell tolls; it tolls for thee.' He's right. The bells were ringing today for all of us, all the citizens of Bay St. Lucy. I don't think I have to go over the details of the tragedy. You have probably all heard them by now. But we simply have to be clear, and state the facts as they are. Miss Royale, whom you see before you here, has lost her mother. Most of us can't think of a more terrible thing for a young person to have happen, but there it is. She's going to have to deal with it, and she is dealing with it. She's a brave girl, a model for us all when grief comes along to us. But now we have to get down to cases. This girl's going to have to have somewhere to live. She's sixteen years old, a minor, and cannot thus live alone. Adoption may be an option down the way, but that's a more time-consuming and legally complex operation than we have time for now. For now, our best option is to find a family that will function in the capacity of her legal guardian. Miss Royale?"

Penelope, realizing that she was being spoken to, seemed to come out of the trance that had masked her features, and said, with a calmer voice than Nina would have thought possible:

"Sir?"

The judge leaned forward on the oaken table behind which he was sitting:

"You cannot know, young lady, how grief-stricken the community is about the tragedy that has befallen your mother and yourself."

"Thank you."

"But you must know that you are not alone. You belong to Bay St. Lucy; you are one of us, and we will help you in every way possible. There are a number of folks here who'd be glad to have you in their home, at least for the next few months, until something more permanent can be worked out. You understand that, do you not?"

Penn seemed to sit higher in her chair.

"Yes, I do. And I appreciate people's concern."

"The city, and with the city the municipal court, will have to formalize the decision of where you are to stay. But never forget that you yourself are going to have a say in this. We're going to try to take all factors into account. But one of the biggest of those factors will be your wishes. So at any time in these proceedings you speak up when you have something to say. Understand?"

"Yes, sir, I understand."

"All right, then, let's start hearing from some people."

And thus began a procession of several speakers: Jenny and Tom Richardson, whose daughter Sarah was five, and who said that Penelope could act as a big sister for the child who—blond-haired and pig-tailed—sat quietly in the audience.

And what kind of a big sister might you turn out to be, Penn? thought Nina, wondering how many four-letter words little Sarah had ever heard in her life.

But the use of profanity—at least in every other word—was a habit Penn was going to have to break.

The Reddingtons had essentially the same arguments to make.

And then—

"I believe the Bannisters would like to speak on this issue.

Nina looked at Frank, who gestured back at her.

All right then, Nina mused.

Class time.

She rose, trying to imagine that everyone in the room was sixteen years old and yearning for the bell to ring. It was her job to hold their attention.

"I think I can be pretty brief. You all know Frank and me. We grew up in Bay St. Lucy. And we can understand at least a little bit of what Penn is going through, because each of us lost parents. Frank's father and mother, as well as mine, were taken by illness, and although it wasn't the same kind of sudden trauma, the unexpected news, that she had to experience yesterday afternoon, loss is loss. We've always looked upon ourselves as lucky because we had each other to help us get through it. Now perhaps we can help Penelope."

The judge breathed deeply, seemed to settle into his chair a bit, and asked:

"Miss Royale is a student of yours, is she not, Nina?"

"She is."

"Miss Royale, do you like Ms. Bannister as a teacher?"

"Yes, sir, I do like her. She makes it interesting."

A smile appeared upon the judge's otherwise stern face, and he said, quietly:

"That is high praise indeed, Nina. I wish I could say that all my English teachers made it interesting."

The same smile spread around the room, remained present for short time, and then evaporated.

"Well, thank you, Bannisters, Frank and Nina. And, of course, you're right. The court knows you well, knew your parents well—as the court knows the Richardsons and the Reddingtons. Any one of these families would make fine caretakers for you, Penelope. Before any decision is to be made on this matter, though, we need to hear from two other people. One is Bruce Thornton and the other is Faye Reed. Mr. Thornton represents Pathfinders from Vicksburg and Ms. Reed is here on behalf of The Learning Tree, an institution based in Meridian."

Foster homes, Nina found herself thinking.

And good ones, of course, she told herself, *or the Judge would not have invited their representatives.*

Both speeches were essentially the same. Penelope would be welcomed with open arms in their institutions. She would have any number of chances to create a social life. The nearby schools were excellent. A high percentage rate of young people in each school received college scholarships, and the schools themselves had some funds available to help toward higher education.

Nina found herself asking one question that would not seem to go away, and, since she and Frank were seated near the back of the room, she was able to lean on his shoulder and whisper it to him:

"What is the difference between these two places?"

He returned the whisper:

"One is pretty expensive; the other is for...."

"Orphans. With no money."

"Yes."

And throughout the remainder of the presentations, as impressive as they were, and as rosy a picture as they painted, she found herself thinking of Dickens and Oliver Twist.

Penelope standing with a bowl in her hand, supplicating some stern headmaster for of bit of extra gruel:

"May I have some more, sir?"

"Penn," she whispered back to Frank, "can't go to one of those places."

Frank merely nodded:

"Court's decision."

"Hasn't the court read *Oliver Twist?*"

"The court didn't have good English teachers; you heard that yourself."

There was nothing to be said to that.

So she turned away and tried not to imagine what Penn was thinking—Penn who, only a day earlier, had said out on the far end of the jetty, "They'll send me to a home, won't they?"

To which she'd answered:

"No, Penn, they won't."

And now, and now, they might.

Court's decision.

But finally the presentations were over, everyone was seated, and the judge was glancing at his watch.

"The court wishes to thank all here for their graciousness, and for the good wishes that these presentations represent. What I think now needs to happen is, I should like to talk briefly and in private with each of the families that have volunteered, to be sure you all know what will be expected of you once a decision has been made. I also wish to speak confidentially with you Ms. Royale. You may, almost certainly do, have wishes in this matter, and it would be unfair to ask you to make those wishes known right now, out loud, on the spur of the moment. I'd like to do these private conversations tonight, because it's still relatively early. But at the present I think we could do with a short recess, just to get our..."

But the short recess did not come.

It was prevented from coming by the opening of the chamber's outer door and the entrance of a tall gaunt figure dressed in blue jeans, suspenders, a green, not very well pressed nor very well tied, tie.

"I'm sorry I'm late, your honor. I got here as quick as I could."

The judge seemed surprised for a moment, but spoke mildly:

"That's all right. Did you have something to add in this matter?"

"I do have something to add. I'd like for Ms. Royale to come and live with me. I'd like to be her father, at least for as long a time as she still needs a father."

"Well, I—well, everyone will get a chance to make a case about this. I think we all know you, sir, but, for the record if you'd tell us—"

"My name, yes, your honor. And, yes, I think everybody here does know me. Just like I know them."

With this, he smiled and said:

"They know me because all of them been fishing with me. Yes, sir, your honor. My name is Lazarus Cousins."

Upon hearing the name, Penelope stood bolt upright, pointed towards the figure standing in the doorway, and said:

"I want to live with him."

The room was paralyzed and, for the next minute at least (although it seemed more), the only thing in Bay St. Lucy capable of the slightest movement at all was the ocean.

Finally some of the shock wore off. People rose, milled around, breathed, and tried to make sense of the situation. Judge Davis did the only thing that he could do, which was to invite Lazarus Cousins, Penelope, Nina and Frank into a smaller chamber, where, in five minutes or so, they all found themselves seated around a small table that could well have been used for poker or bridge.

"Mr. Cousins," began the judge, "the court appreciates your kind offer."

"Yes, sir. It's made with all sincerity. I believe I could do well by Miss Royale. I would take good care of her."

"I'm sure you would. I'm quite sure you would. It's just—"

The sentence stopped in mid-air and hung out over a cliff for a time.

Everybody stared at everybody else.

Finally, the judge, who'd been hanging over the abyss long enough, had no choice but to fall down into it.

"I'm not sure, Mr. Cousins, that it would be appropriate."

"Why," asked Penn, "wouldn't it be appropriate?"

Lazarus Cousins leaned forward on the table.

"Yes, Your Honor. I'd like to know the same thing. Why would it not be whatever was that word you said, *appropriate*?"

"Well, it's just—"

Penn and Cousins together:

"Just what?"

Nina looked at Frank, who seemed to be getting sick. She wondered for a time why the judge had asked the two of them into the chamber, realized it was because she was the smartest person in Bay St. Lucy and Frank was the only lawyer at the meeting, realized also that, being as smart as she was she should've realized that the best thing to do was *shut up*, did shut up, and simply watched as the little piece of theater continued to unfold.

"I'm an honorable business owner, Your Honor, have been for more than thirty years."

"Yes. The court knows that, Mr. Cousins."

"I never been accused of doin' any bad deeds in my life. Nina and Frank can tell, so can lots of folks. I took Nina out fishing with her daddy when she wasn't no more than six years old. That's right; ain't it, Nina?"

The six-year-old Nina awakened within the twenty-two-year-old Nina. She was standing on the deck feeling the wind and riding the swells as the boat did, and both Lazarus Cousins and her father were smiling down at her.

"They were some," she said, quietly, "of the best times in my life."

"And there was times when just you and me went out together. All day sometimes. Your daddy drop you off at the pier in the morning, pick you up at night. Pickle sandwiches. Never could figure that out, Your Honor. This little girl liked to eat pickle sandwiches. So I made them for her, still remember doin' it!"

"I never knew," said Frank quietly, "that you like pickle sandwiches."

"A girl," Nina answered, "has to have her secrets."

Lazarus Cousins looked around the table, breathed deeply, and continued:

"You know, Your Honor. Everybody in Bay St. Lucy knows, I guess. I lost my wife fifteen years ago. She had a heart attack."

Davis nodded:

"I know Lazarus. It was my first year here on the bench."

"My daughter and me got crosswise when she was sixteen. She took herself up to New York. Wanted to live with relatives, wanted to get to know high fallutin' writers and painters and such like. She married young and quick after that, got divorced. We don't see each other. All these things, I figure you know."

"Yes."

"I don't stand here before God and all the angels sayin' I could be a father for Miss Royale here, or that she'd get to be the daughter I don't talk to no more. But there ain't nobody in the town, not the Bannisters, not the Richardsons, not the Reddingtons—that would work harder to take good care of her. I've got to tell you, I saw this girl come close to catching a marlin. A blue marlin that not one man in a hundred could have played. I saw it in her eyes that day. She's a natural fisherman. I need her. I want her to be my crew. There's so much I can teach this girl. And she'll learn it. And she'll love it."

He finished.

Everyone was silent.

The ventilation system, not recognizing an impossible situation even when it was so obvious, continued to hum.

The judge bit his lip, clearly contemplated the million or so things he might say in this situation, chose a terrible one, and said it, anyway:

"I think, Lazarus, that it's a question of propriety."

Penelope leaned forward, weight driving the table an inch or so into the brown carpet:

"What do you mean, Judge?"

"I mean—that is to say—"

Nina felt that she had to speak, and did:

"I think what the judge is trying to say, Penn, is that you need a mother, too."

"My mother's dead, Mrs. Bannister."

More silence.

Then Penelope asked the judge:

"I haven't said much. Can I, now, Your Honor?"

"Of course. Of course, you can."

"All right then. I know that everyone here is out for my best interests. And I appreciate more than I can say the fact that these families are willing to take me in. But I—I'm not like other people. I don't know why God made me like he did. He made me more like a man than a girl. When I was out in Mr. Cousins' boat, it just— well, I just knew. I'll finish high school. I know I need to do that. But I don't want to go to college. That isn't for me. I just want one thing in my life: I want to be the captain of a fishing boat, like Mr. Cousins is."

Silence for a time, then Judge Davis:

"That's a fine ambition, Penelope. And there's nothing wrong with you becoming a kind of hand for Mr. Cousins. We could have an arrangement in which you work for him several hours a day down at the docks. But as for the other matter—"

"What other matter?"

"Well, actually living with him—"

Okay, Nina, you've got to say this, so go ahead.

"It wouldn't look right, Penn."

"Why not?"

"A single man and a young girl…"

"Are people going to think we're having sex?"

"No, no, of course not. It's just…"

"Just what? Mr. Cousins?"

"Yes, Penelope."

"How old are you, if I may ask?"

"Sure you may ask. The Good Lord done let me be here on this earth sixty-eight years."

"Are you planning to rape me or seduce me?"

He smiled and shook his head.

"No. You know I won't do none of those things."

With that, she looked around the room and said, defiantly:

"There. It's in the record. The lady sitting in the corner has written it down. Now why can't I go and live with this man, who has so much to teach me?"

And so it fell to Nina.

She rose, took a deep breath, and said firmly and clearly to both Penn and the rest of the room and the rest of the world:

"Because he's black, Penelope."

And finally, the huge pink elephant in the room stood on its hind legs, trumpeted a braying call through its fifteen-foot-long trunk, and danced on the table.

So it fell to Frank, wonderful Frank, Frank who was about to show everyone why Nina loved him so much, and had always loved him, said quietly:

"That shouldn't matter, Judge."

Davis:

"I know it *shouldn't* matter. After all, this is Mississippi in 1969; there's no racism here!"

"What then is your concern?"

"Well, dammit, people will talk!"

"It's Bay St. Lucy, Your Honor. There aren't that many people here in the first place *to* talk. And those of us who are here are mostly crazy anyway. People who do normal things, live in normal ways—probably wouldn't want to be here in the first place."

"But Frank, don't you see it would be more appropriate for Ms. Royale to live with you and Nina, at least for—"

"We don't want her."

Silence for a time.

Davis:

"You what?"

"We don't want her."

"I don't understand."

"We won't take her. Neither will the Reddingtons nor the Richardsons."

"How do you know that?"

"Because I'll tell them not to take her. And they'll listen. So your only choice would be to send Penelope to one of the two foster homes represented tonight. Penn, you'd go to either of those homes, wouldn't you?"

"Yes."

"And then?"

"I'd run away."

Judge Davis sighed.

Frank:

"The best citizen in Bay St. Lucy, our most upright, our hardest-working, our most honorable, has volunteered to take into his home and train a young woman who has, despite a horrible loss, has seen a vision of what her future is to be like. And you're going to tell him he can't do this. Because *people will talk*?"

Judge Davis thought for a time.

Penelope was leaning forward on the table.

So was Lazarus Cousins.

Finally:

"No. No, Frank, maybe you're right."

Penelope hissed through clenched teeth:

"Yessss!"

Cousins beamed and gave her a thumbs up.

And Penelope grinned at Nina, saying:

"Someday, Mrs. Bannister, I'll be Jamie Hawkins in *Treasure Island.*"

And Nina could do nothing but beam back, feeling a tear come into first one eye, then another, and her unsteady voice whispered back:

"I know you will, Penn. I know you will."

There was then no question about it. Rumors would spread the following day, and a few people would shake their heads and talk about the decline of moral values on the Mississippi Delta (where moral values had, of course, been astonishingly high previously); but Penelope Royale would go and live in the comfortable two-story frame house of Lazarus Cousins. And *tonight*. These two mismatched souls were not lovers, not in any conventional *Lady Chatterley's Lover* way. But in a sense they *were* lovers. They loved the sea, and when Cousins spoke of the need to be at the docks by 4:30 tomorrow morning, Penelope could think of nothing more than switching her bunk, asking Nina to help gather her belongings, and drive to the home of her new Captain My Captain, who would, by the time of their arrival (shortly after ten) have the spare bedroom pristinely clean and ready.

All of this was dutifully done, and by ten-thirty, Nina was pulling the Volkswagen into the Bannister's driveway.

Where Moon Rivard's patrol car sat, lights flashing.

Frank and Moon were talking in the yard.

"Why don't you go on inside, Nina. Officer Rivard is just getting me up to date on a few things. By the way, I made you something to eat. Neither one of us had time for dinner tonight. It's on the counter."

"What is it?"

"Something you'll like. Enjoy it. I'll be right up."

Nina went inside, turned on the small light above the sink, and saw, lying on a paper napkin, the thing Frank had made for her.

A pickle sandwich.

Dill slices on rye, with a bit of mayonnaise.

She had settled into her favorite chair in the living room, and had half-eaten the sandwich, when, through

ाि।ं

the window, she saw Moon Rivard's patrol car driving away.

"So now," said Frank, closing the front door behind him, "you have no more secrets. How is it?"

"It's good."

"I could have used white bread."

"Nope. This is perfect."

"How did the move go?"

"It went wonderfully. I never saw two people more happy about an arrangement."

"Good."

"And Frank…"

"Yes?"

"I was proud of you tonight."

"Why?"

"You know why. You said what needed to be said. People will talk? All right, so let them talk. They're going to talk about Penelope anyway. But she idolized Lazarus Cousins from the first time she saw him. Anybody in the world would have seen that."

She took a final bite of her sandwich, washed it down with a slurp of milk, and then said, quietly:

"It's changing, Frank."

"What is?"

"Penn's life. One tough break after another. And the grief about her mother. But I think the worst is done for her now. It's going to get better."

She set the empty milk glass down, nodded, and said, firmly:

"The worst is done for Penelope."

Frank took a step inside, sighed, and said:

"You think so?"

"I really do."

"Good to hear that. Because Moon just told me about the autopsy reports."

"They're done?"

"Finished up today. The body will be delivered tomorrow."

"That's good."

"Maybe not so good."

She hesitated, looked closely at her husband, and leaned forward:

"What are you talking about, Frank?"

"I'm talking about how the worst is over for Penelope."

"Yes? Why shouldn't it be?"

"Because her mother was murdered."

CHAPTER SIX: KIDNAPPED!

Those who grow up by the sea gravitate to the sea. They are drawn to it, especially in times of great stress or emotional upheaval.

Thus, Nina and Frank found themselves walking on the beach even before they began the discussion that each of them knew must follow hard upon the reception of Moon Rivard's news. They said nothing at all during the putting on of windbreakers, the lacing up of tennis shoes, and the donning of nearly identical flop hats. Was it after eleven o'clock? Well then, so be it.

"I can't believe it, Frank. It doesn't make sense."

"I know."

"Are they certain?"

"Apparently. That's why they took a long time with the autopsy."

The ocean was still the ocean, and the same ocean beside which they'd walked any number of times. But tonight it was different somehow. The water had an oily sheen to it.

"Who murdered her?"

"I don't know."

"Why was she murdered?"

"I don't know that either. But here's what Moon Rivard told me. The Bay St. Lucy police office just got word from New Orleans. The coroner was suspicious when the body was brought it because of bruising."

"What kind of bruising?"

"Neck, shoulders."

The sky, Nina could not help noticing, was different too. The stars could still be seen, but not as distinctly. It was as though a faint scrim had been hung between them and the earth.

"Like she'd been strangled?"

"No, but held, and possibly beaten up."

"Oh God, how can this just keep getting worse and worse?"

"I don't know, but it does. It wasn't just the bruising. There were rope burns."

"Someone beat her, then tied her up?"

"Looks that way. Anyway, all that caused them to look closer at the precise cause of death."

The wind had an edge to it. Not that it was cold exactly, but it was simply different. So was the air pressure. Nina had always been able to sense, even as a little girl, when the barometer had fallen.

"It wasn't a drug overdose?"

"It *was* a drug overdose. But a massive one, not one she might've given herself by accident."

"So someone beat her, tied her to something–"

"They think, apparently, after examining the room, that it must have been a chair."

"All right. Someone beat her, tied her to a chair, and then pumped some kind of drug—"

"Heroin," Frank said, quietly.

"Heroin into her arm until she died."

"That's the situation, apparently."

Storm.

The ocean, the stars, the wind, the air pressure.

A storm was coming.

"Okay then, what happens now?"

"As I understand it, the body is being flown here now, and will arrive early tomorrow morning. Standard procedure calls for it to be examined by our own coroner, who needs to corroborate the New Orleans findings. Then, once the cause of death is officially listed as homicide, both Mississippi and New Orleans police forces will begin a murder investigation."

"This is a nightmare."

She put her arm around him and looked up, watching his face as he pursed his lips and whispered:

"I know."

"How are you involved in all this, Frank?"

They passed a dead fish that had washed ashore.

That, too, was wrong.

What kind of storm would this be?

"I've got to be involved. I've been named by the court as the legal entity most involved in clearing up Ms. Royale's affairs."

"But you don't know anything about her murder."

"Maybe not, but the police don't know that."

"You're not saying they suspect you?"

"Of course they don't. At least I think they don't. But the question is one of money. I have access to her financial records. Those have to be examined to see if she owed anyone."

"Okay, I see that. So what else is involved in a murder investigation?"

"I'm not sure. But then we need to get home. Moon said the police are going to want to get in touch with me. Probably early tomorrow morning, but he couldn't rule out later tonight."

"Wonderful," she said, biting her lip. "Just what we need."

"There's something else we don't need, but we may have to deal with it, anyway."

"All right, hit me with it."

He had put his arm around her shoulder now, and she was glad. The weight of it seemed to comfort her somehow.

"The newspaper. This probably isn't front page material in New Orleans. Stuff like this goes on there pretty frequently. But here in Bay St. Lucy? One of our residents is murdered in a French Quarter motel room? That's front page stuff, bigger even than the Tarpon Festival."

"Don't exaggerate."

"I'm just saying."

"I understand. Does anybody know about this yet?"

Just in front of them three ravenous gulls were tearing at another fish that had been washed up by the oil-slickened ocean.

"Just the police from what I can understand from Moon. But once the body gets here, an announcement will have to be made. Then all hell will break loose. Who knows how many reporters will be swarming around?"

"BAY ST. LUCY PROSTITUTE MURDERED IN SEX TRYST!"

He nodded.

"That's about it, except that most of the people who write this kind of stuff don't know what *tryst* means. Nor do any of the people who read it."

"Frank, who's going to tell Penelope?"

They were twenty feet from the gulls, who didn't seem to notice their approach.

"The police will tell her early tomorrow morning. Then they're going to have to interrogate her."

"Interrogate Penn? Why in heaven's name?"

"Nina, it's a murder investigation. They have to find out everything they can about the woman's activities."

Now ten feet. Now five.

"She was a prostitute, Frank! Prostitution was her activities!"

"I know, but—"

"But what? Do they think Penn was her pimp or what? Clearly she had a—well, a client, who got mad at her. Maybe she wouldn't do what he wanted her to do. They were getting high together, he took the bondage thing a little too far, she told him enough was enough, and he got carried away!"

Cawing confusedly and fluttering their wings, the gulls finally heaved themselves into the air. The shapeless mass of fish meat they'd been devouring was just beside Nina, who didn't look at it.

"Nina, I don't know what to tell you. Probably Penelope's mother died in just that way, or something similar. But clearly the police have to find out everything they can about all her activities during the final days of her life. Maybe she said something to Penelope about a problem she was having, or some guy who was giving her grief. Maybe Penn overheard a telephone conversation. Whatever it might be, they're going to have to interview her."

"All right, all right, I understand."

They walked on for a time.

Finally, Nina:

"What about the funeral?"

"Tomorrow afternoon, I think. It'll be at the Methodist Church. The woman didn't really have any close friends in town, so I'd hoped it would be a fairly small affair. A few people that I'd call tomorrow morning, so she didn't have to be buried alone, her daughter sitting there by herself. No, I'd originally hoped it wouldn't be a big affair."

"But now?" she asked, pulling him closer.

"Now it depends on the newspapers. If the story gets into the afternoon edition of *The Sentinel,* we'll have every Elvis and UFO sighter on the coast packing the place."

"How, oh how, could this get any worse?"

"Only one way that I can think of."

"What way is that?"

"I can't tell you exactly. It's just—"

"Just what?"

"I don't know. I was just thinking it might be worse because of that limousine that's been following us along the beach, and that's now pulling up beside us."

She turned.

Frank was right. The ponderous vehicle, looking like a land-whale, was no more than a few steps behind them, the growl of its engine barely audible because of the soft roar of incoming tide.

"What the hell is going on, Frank? What's that thing doing out here?"

"Taking pictures of the ocean maybe. Or maybe looking for us."

The second answer proved true. The car, a sliver of moon reflecting in its deep black finish, pulled slowly by them, its driver's side tires just skirting the edge of incoming tidewater.

The door opened. A tall, blond-haired, smiling young man got out and spoke to them, saying:

"Mr. and Mrs. Bannister?"

"Yes," Frank answered. "How may we help you?"

The chauffeur—for he seemed to be wearing a chauffer's uniform—opened the back door, gestured into the car, and said:

"I'm here to take you to the airport."

They stood for a second, stock still.

Then Frank looked down at her and said:

"See? *That's* how it could get worse."

The young man continued to smile.

The beach was dead.

No one was out walking. No gulls flew low over the water.

The town was half a mile behind them.

"I beg your pardon?" said one of the Bannisters, it hardly mattered which.

Same smile.

Blue eyes, she could now tell.

Six foot three. This could have been a young football player standing before them.

"The airport. I'm to take you to the airport."

"I don't understand," said Nina.

"The Bay St. Lucy Airport. It's about two miles from here on the other side of—"

"I understand where the airport is. But why are you to take us there?"

"The flight, ma'am."

"What flight?"

"The flight to New Orleans."

"I don't want to go to New Orleans. I don't want to go to the airport."

The young man looked at his watch.

"I hate to insist, but we do need to get on our way. I'm to have you out there before midnight."

"There must," said Frank, taking a step forward, "be some mistake."

"You are the Bannisters, aren't you?"

"Yes."

"Then, no, sir, there's no mistake."

Frank was silent for a time, then said, quietly:

'You're not giving us a choice, are you?"

The young man smiled more broadly, then shook his head:

"No, sir. But we do need to go."

Nina:

"Listen, you can't do this. Who are you? Who do you work for?"

No answer.

Frank:

"He's not going to tell us those things, Nina."

"Well, he *better* tell us those things! I'm not going to get into some car with an absolute stranger and drive off to who knows where! Listen, you, whoever you are! I'm not going, do you understand? You think we're crazy! I'll tell you what I *am* going to do! I'm going home to my house right now, right this very minute! I'm picking up the telephone and I'm calling Moon Rivard. When he comes, you can tell *him* who you are and what all of this foolishness is about, do you understand that?"

"I understand it, ma'am. But we do need to go. There isn't much traffic, so we should make good time. If we leave now."

Silence.

From somewhere in the direction of town, a dog could be heard baying.

The man gestured again.

The black interior of the black car stared out at them.

Nina:

"Frank, are we being kidnapped?"

"Yes."

"Oh, God. What are they going to do to us?"

"I don't know, Nina."

"I could scream."

"We're two miles from the nearest house. One car comes by here every five minutes."

"Do you think he has a gun?"

"I don't think he needs a gun."

"Frank, I have a feeling that if we get into that car, we'll never be seen again. He could take us out into a field, shoot us, and just leave the bodies."

"Yes. Of course, for that matter, he could just shoot us here and roll us into the ocean. Same result. No. We have to go with him. Here. Take my hand."

She did so.

She got into the limousine first. The deep soft dark leather had a smell that, like several other smells that came to her mind, could neither be described nor forgotten.

It was simply the very expensive very new car smell.

Frank followed her in, and the young man carefully closed the car door behind them.

"Frank, I'm scared. I'm really scared."

"I know, honey. I'm scared, too."

"I don't think we should've gotten in."

"We didn't have a choice."

"But—if we're being kidnapped—do you think we'll be held for ransom?"

"No."

"Why not?"

"Because we aren't worth anything."

"Well, I guess that's some comfort."

The car drove two hundred yards back toward Bay St. Lucy, then turned onto a service road that led back to the main highway.

"At least," said Frank, softly, "he's going in the right direction."

He took her hand, squeezed it, and said, quietly:

"Nina, I don't think this guy means to hurt us. There's no reason for anyone to hurt us. We've not done anything to anybody. We're not big time industrialists who could be bartered for a lot of money. Somebody who wanted to rob us back there on the beach would simply have hit us in the head, taken our money. Just hold onto me. It's going to be all right. I don't know what's happening. But trust me—we'll be all right."

She couldn't speak, but holding his hand and burying her face in his windbreaker comforted her. So did the fact that, within five minutes, they'd arrived at the airport.

It seemed almost deserted.

But it was also, she reasoned, not nearly as likely a place to be murdered as the lonely stretch of beach where they'd been walking some minutes before.

Finally, the glass panel separating them from the driver slid open.

His smile had not changed.

She wondered if he'd been smiling at the dashboard for the entire two-mile airport trip.

"Here we are, folks. You can get out now. Just stay where you are, and I'll come back and open the doors.

He did so, helping Nina out first, then Frank.

He then gestured to a small, cream-colored private jet that sat waiting, some fifty yards distant.

The passenger side door of the plane was open, a white metal ramp leading up into it.

"We go there?" asked Frank.

"Yes, sir. Just go right up the ramp. The pilots are waiting on you. Soon as you're in, they'll take off. Y'all have a nice flight to New Orleans."

"Thank you," Nina found herself saying.

Then she kicked herself, mentally.

This was the first time in her life she'd ever been kidnapped and thanked someone for doing it.

What was wrong with her?

Why didn't she just give him candy?

But then, on the other hand, he was so polite!

She shook her head, while walking to the plane.

What in heavens name was going on?

The small private jet was as elegant as the car had been, and just as deserted. Once she and Frank had ascended the ramp and entered the plane, the door was closed behind them. She could hear the ramp being pulled away, as the engines began to roar and the craft moved slowly forward on the taxiway.

Frank was standing in front of her in the dark and narrow fuselage.

"Window seat or aisle?"

"How can you think this is funny?"

"It is funny. We're the last people in the world somebody would want to abduct, and here we are being abducted. But we're being abducted quickly. No stewardess is going to come back from the cockpit and show us how the oxygen mask works. We're just going to take off, fly for forty minutes or so, and land in New Orleans."

"You're sure that's how long it takes?"

He nodded:

"I've made the flight a few times. They barely have time to get to cruising altitude, then they start down. Now, go into that row and sit down. We've got to get buckled in."

She seated herself and fastened the seatbelt.

The jet made one slow turn on the taxiway, stopped for a second or so, then roared off down the runway.

Within seconds they were ascending. Her ears popped; the lights of Bay St. Lucy twinkled below them, and, beyond those Christmas tree light colors, the great dark featureless blanket that was the Gulf.

"Tell me," she said, quietly, "once again how this is going to be okay."

"It's going to be okay."

"You're sure?"

"Yes."

"And the reason you know this is?"

"Because, whoever's responsible for this, if they wanted to hurt us in any way, they would already have done so."

"All right. I believe you. Now, though, if you'll put your arms around me and pull my face over against your chest, there's something I need to do for a few minutes."

"What?"

"Cry."

"All right, come here, my baby."

She did, and then she did.

Her crying, which began as slight dripping from the eyes, turned into seismic sobbing, and the entire eruption lasted at least five minutes.

When she'd finished, Frank's shirt was wet and her tear sockets were dried out.

He said a few things to comfort her, but her breath was coming in short, convulsive heaves, and she could only nod or shake her head at what seemed appropriate times.

She turned away after a time, feeling somewhat ashamed of herself, and pressed her nose against the window glass.

The lights that she could see now were tiny dots of white and blue and occasional red, but thicker clouds were scudding beneath them, and she remembered reading in the local paper that a hurricane was forming over Cuba, and that weather patterns might be disrupted.

Unseasonable rains up and down the coast affected Louisiana and Mississippi.

Finally, when she could speak reasonably well, she said:

"I'm sorry I'm acting this way, Frank."

"Don't be sorry. But you need to get your mind off all of this."

"We're walking down a beach two miles away from Bay St. Lucy; a huge black limousine that looks like a hearse pulls up by us and tells us to get in, refusing to tell us anything but that we're being taken—against our will, that is, *kidnapped*—to New Orleans. We don't know who's planned this, or what we're expected to do when we get to New Orleans, or if we'll have a place to stay, or where that place will be, or how we'll get there. We don't know one soul in Bay St. Lucy who knows our whereabouts. And these are the things you want me to get my mind off? What would you prefer that I think about?"

"Well, you could think about the fact that, whatever is happening to us, we're going to know about it soon. We're going down."

He was right. She could feel the nose of the plane tilting downward, and her ears popping again.

The descent was rapid. Before she could decide whether she wished to cry again or not, they were bouncing on the runway.

Two minutes later, they heard the door open behind them and saw the garish glare of airport lights illuminating the tube that was the cabin.

Rain, they could hear, was pelting the tarmac.

Within a minute of the door's opening, the ramp rattled and yet another chauffeur appeared, this one a young black man, precisely the same height and build as the one who'd stopped them on the beach.

A heavy yellow water-glistening parka only partially covered his uniform.

"The Bannisters?"

Frank answered:

"Yes."

"I'm to give you this letter, then drive you down into the Quarter. Sorry about the rain tonight. Apparently there's a hurricane out there somewhere. I have trench coats for you in the car, and some overshoes for you to wear."

Frank, who was still seated on the aisle, took the ivory-colored envelope that was offered to him, tore it open, and held it beneath the reading light in the panel above them.

The handwriting was elegant, and seemed, Nina found herself thinking, to have been written with a true ink pen and not a ballpoint.

She read:

A SERIOUS PROBLEM HAS ARISEN, AND ONE, I FEEL, THAT THE TWO OF YOU ARE UNIQUELY QUALIFIED TO HELP SOLVE. I HAVE THUS VOLUNTEERED YOUR SERVICES TO A GROUP OF BUSINESS ASSOCIATES. MY REGRETS AT THE INCONVENIENCE, AND AT THE FACT THAT YOU WILL BE REQUIRED TO WALK IN INCLEMENT WEATHER. THE ONLY CONSOLATION I CAN OFFER YOU IS THAT, SHOULD YOU BE SUCCESSFUL, YOU WILL BE GENEROUSLY COMPENSATED.
SINCERELY YOURS,
HOMER BARON ROBINSON

She finished reading the letter, then looked at Frank and said:

"This is all your fault."

He sighed.

CHAPTER SEVEN: THE HAUNTED QUARTER

Rain had pounded New Orleans all night, and now, as street lamps glowed and the east wind swung the old wooden hanging signs of the French Quarter, the street lay half submerged in water.

Sounds of car horns, sirens, revelers, and mournful jazz records mixed with the roaring of the wind and the soft plashing of pedestrians' feet crossing the puddles. Most of that noise, Nina knew, came from Bourbon Street, several blocks west of them. But they were walking on Royal Street now, in a part of the Quarter less frequented by late revelers, and secretive, shuttered windows flowed past her like water in the gutters, windows that kept their part of the bargain not to look out at her if she did not look into them.

There are many myths concerning New Orleans' French Quarter, most of them untrue, but none more deceptive than the notion that the entire area is now nothing more than a theme park; that mystery and romance have essentially vanished, and that behind the black grillwork and glowing street lanterns there lie only tourists.

But the quarter has other people, too: genuine ghosts, who seldom see the light of day, and inhabit places long since forgotten by the real estate agents and never glimpsed by fun seekers.

Nina followed Frank onto Barrack Street, which was completely deserted. The rain bored on, harder now, colder, slanting, driven by the wind into her face. Ten yards, twenty yards—she twisted her neck, peered back behind her, saw no one following. There were no shops now, no antique stores or bars or jazz clubs. Only implacable grillwork and tightly shut doors, the balconies overhead deserted, the entire narrow street little more than an alleyway, dark except for the occasional faintly glowing lamp behind a dusty window.

Frank turned, shouting above the noise of the storm:

"We're close now!"

"What was the address he gave you?"

"One hundred and ten, Barracks Street."

"You've got the key?" she asked.

"Right here in my pocket!"

"Why in God's name couldn't the guy have just *driven* us there?"

"I have no idea. But then Homer Baron Robinson does business in his own way."

"We never should have gotten mixed up with that man, Frank!"

"I have to admit, the wetter and colder I get, the more inclined I am to agree with you."

"Good that you've finally seen the light; just a bit too late it seems."

"All right, all right! Come on, let's find this place and see if we can get out of the storm!"

He turned and they walked on.

Fifty yards more and they'd reached their destination.

An old, wooden, faded sign swung above them:

FRENCH QUARTER MAISONETTES

"This," she shouted, "is a hotel of some kind."

Frank, pulling the ponderous metal key from his pocket, shook his head:

"It *was*. If the rest of the place is in the same condition the sign is in, it hasn't been inhabited for twenty years."

She pressed her forehead against the wet-cold grating, and peered into the deserted garden area that had apparently once served as an entrance hallway for the French Quarter Maisonettes.

She could see nothing but dark shapes: a table here, a metal chair there, all of it rusting now for a decade or more, all of it serving as mausoleum rather than habitation.

Frank slid the key into the door's lock, twisted it, waited for and heard the *click* sound, and pushed the gate open.

It creaked as it swung.

He walked through and she followed, then, not knowing precisely why, stuck her head back onto the street to look both ways.

Nothing moved but a dog, a mongrel, prowling from alley to alley, attempting to find some garbage that the specters living now in these lost streets might have cast aside.

Frank slammed the gate shut behind them and locked it.

They walked on into the garden/entryway which was, thankfully, covered by a kind of dull, Plexiglas roof.

Rain drummed hard above them but, at least, she thought, it was no longer pelting into them.

A door opened from a balcony to their right, and out of it, stopping just at the rickety rail, wobbled the dwarfian image of a woman.

"Hallo, mes cheres! Pauvre chers! Toute mouillant, comme vous êtes!"

The figure peering down at Nina was not more than five feet tall. Atop it was a face that could have been a caramel apple, to which a sharp needle could have been taken, making innumerable narrow slits which most people would now have called wrinkles.

"We don't," said Nina, "speak French."

The woman smiled:

"Oh, I so apologize! I forget my manners. So few come in these times. I forget the speaking of English! I merely say that I am sorry for you, who are so wet. Take off your big plastic coats and shoes! I shall bring down towels, and something warm for you to drink. Oh, and I should tell you, I am Madame Darrouzes."

So saying, she disappeared.

Finally, Nina said:

"This place gives me the creeps. Those vines and tangled up palm leaves—it seems like we're in a jungle, but one that nobody's touched for a decade or so."

"A haunted hotel."

"Frank, what in God's name is going on here? What kind of *serious problem* could Homer Baron Robinson have that we could possibly help him to solve? And what does this weird place have to do with it?"

"I don't know. I keep thinking we'll find out soon what's going on. But we don't, and things just keep getting crazier and crazier."

"We could leave. Before that old woman comes back, we could run."

"Run where? Back out into the rain?"

"There are worse things than rain."

"So where would we go? We have no money except for a five dollar bill I've been carrying around all day."

"We could go to a hotel or something and call the police."

"And tell them what? Please save us, we've been flown to New Orleans in a private jet, owned, probably, by one of the richest men on the Gulf Coast? They'd think we were drunk."

"*I'm* beginning to think we're drunk. Except I'm not enjoying it."

"I understand what you're saying. But I still think if we just—"

He was interrupted by the re-appearance of gnome-like Madame Darrouzes, who came toddling forth out of a thicket of fern leaves as though she were some bush animal creeping out of the Amazon jungle into a clearing.

"Here, my babies. Nice dry towels. I have robes inside if you would like for to wear them in your meet up."

"I think I'll just keep on my sweater and jeans," said Nina. "The raincoats kept out most of the water."

"What meet up?" asked Frank, somewhat to the displeasure of Nina, who was not at all sure she wanted to know.

"De one with Mr. Johnson. He in the dining room now, finishing his meal."

"Who," asked Frank, "is Mr. Johnson?"

"Oh, a very important man he is."

"Does he work for Homer Baron Robinson?"

Madame Darrouzes shook her clay-apple head, disturbing wisps of gray hair that were matted on top of it.

"Me I don't know such a person. But dey are so many of them. Dey come from all different countries. Sometime when two or three of them meet up here, I don't get a word dey say. Different colors dey are and different sizes. Sometimes men, sometimes women."

Nina heard a sound from what seemed, judging from the darkened window to her left, to be a larger room.

"Dat's de bell he uses. He likes bells. Was a sea captain, so he tell me. Tells time wid the bell. Two bells, tree bells, you know how dey do it, when out on de ocean. Come, you follow me."

She moved off and the two of them went just behind her, aware that the rain was beating even harder now on the Plexiglas ceiling.

"No," she croaked over her shoulder, "dey all different. Just one ting dey have that is the same. One thing you can't miss. About all of them."

"What is that?" asked Frank.

"De smell. Dey all have the same smell."

"What smell?"

She turned and smiled:

"Why, de smell of death."

Then she opened the door in front of her, said, "You go in now and have de talk with Mr. Johnson."

And she disappeared back into the rain forest.

They stepped into what had obviously once been the dining room of the old hotel. It was dark and musty now, though, and Nina thought that, should there have been light enough to illuminate the upper corners, they would have been shrouded in cobwebs.

What light there was came from a table across the room, upon which burned a candelabra sprouting four small flames. To the side of this golden trident, sat a hulking figure with white shirt open at the collar, black unkempt and tangled hair, and a dazzling white smile that was the noon sun to his raven/coal midnight hair.

"Come! Come forth!" he croaked, in what Nina immediately took to be a kind of near-cockney accent. "The Good Madame Darrouzes has brought ye to me— now come farther, that I may take the measure of those that I be dealing with!"

They each took two steps forward, hearing and feeling the old board floor creak beneath their weight.

Other than that sound, and the rattling of rain on the roof, there was nothing to hear except the hissing of candle flames.

"Aye. You're still a bit soggy from the big blow I see. Apologies for that, can't be helped, can't be helped. Hurricane out there somewhere, forming fast they say. Sorry you had to walk. The organization frowns it does on automobile traffic near the rooms here. People walking in from time to time, why, that's to be accepted. But people don't wear numbers, which automobiles do, and can by that feature be identified. I hopes you understand."

They did not understand, of course, but neither had they understood anything for the last hours, and there was nothing to do but stand and wait.

The figure got to its feet.

Seeing him do that was an unforgettable show in itself, for the pure rising and expanding took twice the time, Nina told herself, that an ordinary man would require.

He was huge. And if he'd been, as the woman pointed out, a lover of the sea, his shirt alone, expanded by his massive chest, could have been the mainsail of a galleon.

"Johnson. Ye may call me Mr. Johnson. Today that is!"

His smile broadened.

"Tomorrow. Tomorrow and tomorrow and tomorrow, why then may it be Brown or Green or even Pink were there to be conceived of such a being as Mr. Pink. But sit! Sit, the two of ye! Take the burden off your feet, at that small table beside where ye now stand."

They did. Then he unfurled himself and eased back down into the only oaken chair in the hall strong enough to support him.

He was drinking, Nina could see, from a small flask; a bony ribcage lay on the otherwise empty platter beside him.

"Do ye take with rum? I have enough here to offer each of you a splash. If more is needed, then the good madam can always get some."

Frank, making an effort, was finally able to speak.

"We're fine."

"All right then. Fine it is. Too late for dinner and spirits anyway unless ye be old Mr.—what did I say, Johnson? Yes, unless ye be he and then are all bets off!"

He sipped again from the flask, wiped his bearded mouth with a yard or so of his sleeve, and then growled:

"The two of you come recommended."

There seemed nothing to say to that. "Recommended by whom?" would be one possible reply, but Nina didn't make it, thinking that it would come on its own.

"The good Mr. Robinson—"

There it was.

"—the good Mr. Robinson speaks highly of ye."

"Homer Robinson?" asked Frank, uselessly.

How many Robinsons did they know, anyway?

"Aye, the Baron, the Baron. Not a dues-paying member of our—well, our corporation, let's call it—but a knowledgeable man, and one whose advice need oft be listened to. He says ye can be depended upon. That ye be discreet. And that ye be, both of ye, in unique positions to help us with the problem. The problem, the problem. The time has come, the walrus said, to speak of many things. Of cabbages and kings. And of—for we shall have to get round to speaking of the poor lady at some time or other and why should it not be now, no, why indeed?—the poor deceased Mrs. Royale."

The name floated across the room like a ghost, hovered for a time, then evaporated, leaving a scent, which Nina now realized was the same scent emitted by the hulking figure that sat before them.

The scent of death.

Penelope's mother.

Somewhere in the back of Nina's mind—during the abduction on the beach, the jet ride, and the walk through a besodden and haunted French Quarter—was the notion that the murdered woman and her daughter might be involved in all of this.

She had though, she supposed, attempted to block out the possibility.

"You know, Mr. Bannister—Bannister, Bannister. Fine name, old Cornish name, I think, and, yes, I knew a bosn's mate of the name once—you know, I take it, some of the circumstances surrounding the lady's demise."

Frank nodded and said, quietly:

"She was apparently murdered."

"Aye, that she was. An unfortunate thing. But naught can bring her back to us now. Possessed of a daughter, I believe she was."

"Yes," Nina heard herself saying. "The girl's name is Penelope."

"Penelope. Lovely name. Wife of that great old sailor Odysseus. Soul of fathfulness and true love. Thwarter of the suitors, blackguards all, they. Penelope."

"I'm still not certain—"

Frank began but was cut off:

"No, of course, you be not, nor how would you be? Dragged here in the middle of the night in the worst rain of the year, but not complaining, neither of you, yea, old Baron Robinson knows the mettle of the folk he recommends! No, of course, not certain, not certain."

A pause, then:

"Well, I suppose then that it may now be time to make you more certain. And so the matter at hand is merely this. We are told that you, Mr. Barrister

Bannister, are the de facto executor of the lady's estate."

"Yes, the court made that appointment."

"You pay her bills, so to speak."

"Yes."

"Well, then, now we come to the problem. The problem."

"I've tried to deal with all the bills I could learn of, her back rent, her car—"

"But there is, you see, a bill you have not learned of. And this bill, well, unfortunately, it must be paid."

"How much is the bill?"

"In pounds or dollars?"

"Dollars."

"Ah, then—dollars, that would be—oh hang the technicalities of the matter, why quibble over exact numbers? A close approximation would be—a million and a half of them."

She and Frank sat open mouthed.

Outside, a dog began to bay.

CHAPTER EIGHT: THE TRANSPORTER OF GOODS

The dog had been baying for some time when Nina attempted to speak, and failed. She wasn't sure why no sounds were coming out of her mouth, since her lips, she could feel, were definitely moving.

So it was Frank who managed to deliver the Barrister Bannisters' first official response to the news that Eva Royale owed somebody—and probably somebody quite dangerous—a million and a half dollars.

"What was that number you said?"

"A million and a half. Give or take, you understand."

"That's impossible."

"Nevertheless."

Finally, Nina found her voice. She leaned forward on the table before her and almost shouted:

"Eva Royale didn't have a cent to her name! She and her daughter were living in poverty! If she had a million and a half dollars, why was she turning tricks to support her drug habit? She was almost certainly killed by one of her *customers* who wanted more than she could give him, and who tied her up and gave her an overdose because he was strung out and mad."

Johnson shook his head, which made his great body shake, which in turn shook everything else in the room.

"Alas, dear lady, an interesting theory, but not a true one."

Nina:

"And a true one would be?"

"She was killed by one of my associates."

"You know the murderer?"

"I do."

And then it happened again, of course, lips moving, no sound coming out.

Why, she asked herself, *did that keep happening*?

But then she looked around her, remembered where they were, and also remembered what had happened to them. Was happening to them.

That was why it kept happening.

"Who," asked Frank, softly, "killed her then?"

Another shake of the head, more resulting shakes of the general topography and attached furnishings.

"I said I know, Mister Frank Bannister, of, I am relatively certain, Cornwall descent. I did not say, though, that I chose to tell."

Frank persisted:

"Okay. But you are planning to tell us something, I guess, and that something should have to do with *why* she was killed."

"Excellent! The nail on the head, as it were! She was killed due to unacceptable irregularities in her handling of goods."

"Her handling of—"

But finally, Nina understood, and said what was going to have to be said at some point anyway.

"Heroin."

"Precisely, my dear, precisely."

Frank:

"Eva Royale was smuggling heroin?"

Johnson:

"Carrying it, to be most precise. Carrying it, from one place to another."

"So why did this get her killed?"

"It got her killed, my dear sir, because of the way that she did it. You see, concerned as she must have been for the ultimate financial welfare of herself and her young daughter, she decided to go into business for herself."

"How," asked Nina, "was she planning to do that?"

Johnson merely shrugged:

"She planned to do it with the aid of three minor associates—technicians, chemists, etc."

"Are they," Frank asked, "dead now too?"

"I know only that they are buried. I can only hope, for their sakes, that they are also dead."

"So she had a plan to—"

"Dilute higher grade heroin and substitute lower. A little at a time, over a period of several months. She'd hoped to accumulate a—well, I believe that *stash* is the proper word—take the stash, pay off her co-workers, and disappear."

"But it didn't work."

"It did not."

"Because?"

"Because she was stu—no! No, not to speak ill of the departed. Because she was somewhat lacking in business acumen."

"Your gang found out what she was doing, and one of them murdered her."

"We be hardly a *gang*, Mister Bannister. We be a multinational corporation."

"Sorry. I guess I'm just naïve."

"*Gangs* hang around on street corners."

"And you hang around in abandoned hotels."

"You have wit, sir. I appreciate that in a man."

"Good. We're growing on each other."

"That we are. Yes, that we are."

"We still don't understand," said Nina, "what it is that you want us to do."

"We don't," added Frank, "have a million and a half dollars!"

Johnson's eyes brightened:

"But you soon will have!"

"What?"

"Or, that is, you soon will have merchandise worth a million and a half dollars."

"Merchandise?"

"The stash, my dear Bannister. The stash."

A gust of wind rattled palm fronds machine-gun-like against the window, glowing dimly behind Johnson.

Nina, finally understanding, said in little more than a whisper:

"All the top grade heroin she substituted bad stuff for, she kept in one place."

"That she did, m'lady. That she did."

"Do you know where that place is?"

"That we do, m'lady. That we do."

"How do you know?"

"Because she felt it wise to disclose the information to my associate, before she died."

"She thought it would save her life, but it didn't."

"Alas, no."

"So," asked Frank, "if you know where the heroin is, why don't you just go and get it?"

"Because we cannot."

"Why not?"

"Because the police would prevent us from doing so."

"I don't—"

But Nina did.

"Are you saying that Eva Royale was keeping a million and a half dollars' worth of heroin in her house?"

"I am; she did."

"That's crazy," said Frank.

Nina shook her head:

"No. Doing anything else would have been crazy. What was she going to do, Frank, put it in the bank? Here, First Savings and Loan of Bay St. Lucy, is a cellophane bag. It's about the size of a loaf of Wonder Bread, but that stuff in it isn't flour. It's heroin; it's worth over half a million dollars, and please rent me a nice safe deposit box."

"Okay, I guess I can see that."

"She must have thought she was pulling off a perfect scam. She had three clever people working with her. Who would want to search her house?"

"The police," said Frank, quietly. "Later on tomorrow morning."

"Indeed. There are, in fact, yellow *crime scene* ribbons around it as we speak. Forensics experts will be going over every inch of it tomorrow morning, in search of any piece of information that might point to her murderer."

"They'll find the drugs."

"And we shall lose our money. An outcome we hardly wish to see transpire. So, this is where the two of you come in. We are informed, Mrs. Barrister Bannister, that you have already entered the house once."

"Yes. Earlier this evening to help Penn get some things that she needed."

"And so, arriving early this morning—for your plane awaits you—you simply arrive at the house, inform whatever officers you find guarding it in preparation for tomorrow morning's inspections that Ms. Royale needs 'a few more things.'—and go and get our little treasure."

"Which is where?"

"Lying on the top shelf of Ms. Royale's clothes closet, beneath a blue sweater."

"My God. A million and a half dollars on the top shelf of a clothes closet."

"Beneath, as I said, a blue sweater. I believe the bag is in a leather attaché case. Now, as for you, Mr. Bannister, you will accompany your charming wife. A popular attorney, friend of the police chief, executor of Ms. Royale's estate—if any legal problems arise, I feel you will have no difficulty in surmounting them."

Silence for a time.

Wind, rain, siren, dog.

Finally, Johnson:

"Now. Be ye clear on what is expected of ye?"

Frank nodded:

"We're clear. But if we refuse—"

Johnson merely laughed:

"Oh, ye would never refuse! A beautiful young couple with your lives before you? No, no, let us not talk of folly."

Then he said, more quietly:

"There has been quite enough folly involved in the matter, as it is. We do not wish for anything untoward to happen to either of you fine people."

Then, almost growling:

"Or to young Penelope."

Nina:

"You'd kill Penn?"

To which Johnson answered immediately:

"We wants our treasure! And we wants it today! Clear about that, are we?"

Silence for a time, then Frank:

"What do we do with the case when we get it?"

"Take it and go home. Someone will come for it."

"How do we know you won't kill us then?"

"Oh come now. What would be the point of our doing such a thing? To despoil a village of two of its most prominent citizens? We are not, after all, gangsters!"

"Why," asked Nina, "do I keep forgetting that?"

"Ha! Your missus has wit, too, Barrister Bannister! A lucky man you are. And even more fortunate, since a lovely pay check awaits you for your efforts, as I believe Mr. Baron Robinson has informed you already."

Nina shook her head:

"We don't want any money. Not for something like this."

But Johnson shook his head, too, creating much more of a seismic event:

"The money will be there for you, my dear Nina, and you must take it. If not, it will be asked about, and that will create yet another problem. If you do not wish any of it yourselves, and only wish to establish a kind of trust fund for Ms. Royale, then so be it. But do not take it to the police, or—"

Nina interrupted:

"I know."

She did not know.

But she could imagine.

CHAPTER NINE: JUST A FEW MATTERS TO ATTEND TO FIRST

Their flight reached Bay St. Lucy around sunrise, except that sunrise could not be seen because of the heavy rains. She remembered oldsters about the town warning of a bad hurricane season, and for a time she let both her eyes and imagination wander upon the sea, trying simultaneously to remember and to forget what it could do.

The limousine met them at the airport as she knew it would.

It crawled through early morning Bay St. Lucy streets that were almost completely deserted, and, with its glass panel in front of them and dark bulletproof windows—she was sure they were bulletproof, how could they not be?—she felt protected from the world.

She felt thankful for this because she'd never before in her life felt the need of so much protecting, from a world that contained so much to be protected from.

But this womblike enclosure did make it possible for her to talk with Frank, and in a way they hadn't done in the plane.

She didn't know why they'd been so silent on the return flight.

Probably because they knew this conversation was coming, and they didn't look forward to it.

"All right," she said, quietly. "So what do we do?"

"There's only one thing we can do, as far as I can see. This guy's going to take us home. We'll have an hour to get to that house and find the heroin before the forensics team gets there. So that's what we'll do."

She was silent for a time, then asked:

"Who are these people, Frank? Who are we really dealing with?"

"They're part of a very big organization, and that's about all we're ever going to learn about them. But as for now, I feel as though I can predict what's going to happen. We're going to be taken home. We're not even going to go inside. We're just going to get in our little car and go over to the Royales'. What time is it now, seven o'clock? Whatever the police do in that house will start at around eight."

"How do you know that?"

"Moon Rivard told me yesterday evening. A forensics team from New Orleans is flying in. It'll take them at least that long to get here and get set up. There will be a few officers there now, but not too many. One of them will be a woman. Trudy Parker, Mary Thompson—you know the women police officers here in town."

"I think I do."

"Talk to one of them if possible. Tell them that it was so confused and hectic last night you forgot some items Penelope absolutely must have this morning. Toiletries, a tooth brush, I don't know, things women have to have in the morning. I'm sure she'll let you in. Once you do get in, you go back to Eva's bedroom, look on the top shelf of the closet, check under the sweater, and get the attaché case."

"What if she follows me back to the bedroom?"

"I'll distract her."

"How?"

"I'll make love to her."

"Nice that you've still got a sense of humor."

"They say that's the last thing that goes."

"Well I'll treasure it then."

Five minutes later, having been dropped at home by the limo driver, they were preparing to get into their Volkswagen.

Which they were stopped from doing.

"Frank, there's a car pulling up!"

"I see it."

"Are they coming here?"

"I think so."

"It's got a big *five* written across the door."

"That's Curt Parker from Channel Five News."

The car pulled in and stopped. Two men emerged, one holding a TV camera.

Within a minute, they were in the house, drying themselves off.

"Frank and Nina! Bad rain, isn't it? They still don't know where the hurricane's going."

"Yeah, we were just getting ready to get some supplies in, in case it comes this way and not toward Florida. How can we help you, Curt?"

Curt Parker, tall, gangly, sandy-haired and perennially plaid-shirted, smiled his broad smile:

"I got a call about one this morning. They told me what had happened. It's all over town by now. We'd like to tape an interview with the two of you and get it on the Afternoon News."

Damn, thought Nina.

It had to happen. The whole thing had to come to light.

But so soon?

Penelope had probably not even learned yet that her mother had been murdered. That delicious fact would be disclosed to her by the police, probably in an hour or so. The same police who should've been keeping the story scrupulously under wraps.

And then, a scant few more hours later, she'd hear about and see the whole thing on television.

What wonderful beings, she mused, that journalists were.

"Do you mind if I interview you for TV?"

"No. Go ahead."

The camera started whirring.

"Frank, this is the biggest story that's hit Bay St. Lucy in a long time. Maybe ever. I was able to learn that you and Nina are right in the middle of it."

Frank shook his head.

"I'm not sure that's true."

It *was* true, of course. But what was Frank going to say? Yes, it's true. Eva Royale didn't die of a simple drug overdose. The fact is, she was murdered. And she was not murdered by a *john*—(What was Nina doing even using such terms, anyway? She was a high school English teacher, not Raymond Chandler!)—by a *john* who'd gotten too high himself and thus out of control. No, she was murdered by a professional assassin working for an international drug cartel, because she'd attempted to get rich by stealing large quantities of the highest grade heroin.

"What's your opinion, Frank, of the events that have just transpired?"

"We're still trying to make sense of them ourselves."

"You and Nina are both natives of Bay St. Lucy. Has anything similar to this ever happened here in your memory?"

"No, not in mine."

"Nor mine," chimed in Nina.

Who was continuing in her mind the narrative of what really happened, and was happening.

The narrative that had related:

She was murdered by a professional assassin who tortured her sufficiently to find out where she'd hidden a million and a half dollars' worth of heroin, which now was waiting patiently for her and Frank to get it out of the damned bedroom closet.

Now *that* was a narrative.

That was the stuff of Pulitzers!

But probably not the stuff that should be related to a local television reporter at seven o'clock in the morning (They had until eight to get to the Royale's house—then the police would be there.)—by Frank.

Who instead simply said:

"It's all very tragic."

"Were you shocked when this happened?"

"Of course. We both were. The entire town was."

"What do you think will be the effect when Bay St. Lucy learns of it?"

"Again, I can only say shock."

"Frank, we all know this kind of thing goes on in cities like New Orleans."

"Yes, of course we do."

"But here? Bay St. Lucy?"

"I know. It's almost impossible to fathom."

"Do you think there will be violence here in Bay St. Lucy because of it?"

Frank shook his head while Nina simply found herself thinking:

There will only be violence if we can't get over to that damned house in forty minutes. Now finish this interview and let us for God's sakes go!

"There are violent people in the world, Curt. So far, Bay St. Lucy hasn't seen many of them. Nina and I can only hope that it stays that way."

"All right Frank, Nina—thank you for talking with Channel Five."

"Our pleasure."

Curt Parker turned, so that he was facing the camera.

Nina could hear it whirring as he said to the lens, and to the waking village:

"And there you have it, ladies and gentlemen: the opinions of Frank and Nina Bannister, who were and are front and center, in one of the biggest and most shocking stories to unfold in our community this year: a young girl, sixteen-year-old Penelope Royale, mother dead of an overdose of drugs in New Orleans—this young girl has been placed officially, by edict of our own city council, in the home of a sixty-eight-year-old fisherman—who is black! A curious tale indeed, and one whose consequences remain untold. Thank you, Frank! Thank you, Nina! This is Curt Parker, sending it back to the studio!"

He finished speaking.

The camera was put away.

There were perfunctory good byes.

And Frank and Nina were left standing on their porch, watching the rain.

CHAPTER TEN: A FEW MATTERS TO ATTEND TO SECOND

They soon found themselves in the middle of their own living room, staring dumbfoundedly at each other.

They spoke at such a rapid fire pace that none was sure who'd said what:

"Are you kidding me?"

"He didn't even *know* about the murder!"

"This was all about that meeting last night!"

"Thank God, Penelope won't have to see the whole thing about her mother's murder on television."

"No, she'll just have to read about how shocked the town is that she's living with a black man."

There was a pause, during which Nina was able to figure out that it was she indeed who spoke next:

"Frank, maybe we made a mistake."

"Yeah, we didn't go on vacation in Tibet last month."

"No, I mean it."

"So do I. We could have been Dali Llamas by now, whatever those are."

"Maybe we should have taken Penn in, after all."

He shook his head:

"Why? Because we're scared of a few racists?"

"No, because we're scared of a lot of racists."

"Okay, okay, but I don't have time to be scared of *any* racists right now."

"Why not?"

"Because the only time I have, I have to use being scared of drug dealers."

She was silent for a time, then said quietly:

"Yeah. There is that."

"We still have forty minutes. But we need to get over there."

"I'm not sure if we can get over there."

"Why not?"

"Because if you'd turn around and look behind you, through the front door and out at the driveway, you'd see that Adelia Wickersley is getting out of her new Oldsmobile.

He did, and, it was true, she was.

"What in heaven's name," he asked, "is your principal doing here?"

Nina shook her head:

"She could be coming over to offer me a raise in pay. Or even a promotion."

"Right."

"It was just a suggestion."

"Nina, Adelia Wickersley not only has never been in our house—she's never even been in this part of town."

"This might work in our favor, though, Frank."

"How?"

"Maybe we could kill her and give her to the drug dealers."

"The drug dealers don't want her."

"You keep rejecting all my suggestions."

"Well, I'm just in a bad mood today. I don't know why."

"Open the door, Frank."

"I don't want to."

"You have to."

He did, and Adelia Wickersley was soon walking into the Bannisters' living room.

And then the principal was sitting on their couch, smiling and refusing coffee, *thank God* thought Nina, because they had no coffee to offer her anyway other than a pot that they'd have to make, which they had no time to do.

"I'm so sorry to bother you at this early time, Nina."

"That's quite all right. Frank and I have been up for some time."

Oh boy, have we.

"It's just—well, there's aa situation that has arisen that is relatively delicate."

"Oh?"

"Yes, and in my position as your employer, I have been asked to discuss it with you."

Uh oh.

Uh oh uh oh uh oh Uh oh uh oh uh oh Uh oh uh oh uh oh Uh oh uh oh uh oh Uh oh uh oh uh oh Uh oh uh oh uh oh Uh oh uh oh uh oh Uh oh uh oh uh oh Uh oh uh oh uh oh Uh oh uh oh uh oh Uh oh uh oh uh oh Uh oh uh oh uh oh Uh oh uh oh uh oh Uh oh uh oh uh oh Uh oh uh oh uh oh Uh oh uh oh uh oh

"A situation?"

"Yes, my dear."

"Involving?"

"Your home room student, Miss Royale."

"Yes, of course. Well, Penn has had a tragedy occur in her life."

Adelia Wickersley nodded:

"I'm, of course, well aware of that. As is the entire community."

Nina glanced at the circular clock on their living room wall.

They now had twenty-five minutes.

Adelia Wickersley continued.

"And all of us are, as you can imagine, deeply sympathetic, and concerned for the child's welfare."

Like hell you are, Nina thought.

"I'm certain you are," Nina said.

"The problem is, a number of people I've spoken to feel that, in the town's haste to provide a good place for her to stay as she works through her grief, a crucial decision may have been made too quickly, and without proper consideration of all relevant aspects."

"You're talking about the town meeting last night."

"Yes, Nina, I am."

"You weren't at the meeting?"

"No, I was unable to attend. I've been informed this morning concerning certain of its decisions."

"You're talking about the one concerning Lazarus Cousins."

"Yes, the colored fisherman."

Nina nodded:

"Adelia, there was a good deal of debate."

"So I heard. But the number of people at the meeting was, well, quite limited."

"Judge Davis and several families who'd volunteered to take Penn in."

"And you and your husband were one of these families?"

"Yes. Originally."

"Meaning?"

"We decided," said Frank, "to withdraw our offer."

Adelia Wickersley turned and looked at him:

'Oh? And may I ask why?"

Frank:

"Because Penelope obviously wanted to live with Cousins."

"The colored man."

"The good man. One of the best, when you come down to it, that we have here in Bay St Lucy."

Adelia Wickersley looked down at the carpet.

Seemingly finding nothing there to contemplate for a longer period of time, she raised her head and said:

"None of the people to whom I have spoken, have the slightest thing against Mr. Cousins, Mr. Bannister."

Except one, thought Nina.

Except one.

"But the separation of races is a scriptural reality. And one we must accept."

Frank said nothing to this.

Neither did Nina.

"Going to school together is one thing, you both understand. That battle has been fought in the last years of this decade, and I think all our citizens have tried to live as the court's decision would have them live. But living in the same house, as members of the same family—that is something entirely different. I'm sure you both remember Judge Bazile's ruling from January 6, 1959. But if not, I believe that I can quote it: "Almighty God created the races white, black, yellow, malay and red, and he placed them on separate continents. And but for the interference with his arrangement there would be no cause for such marriages. The fact that he separated the races shows that he did not intend for the races to mix."

To which Frank answered:

"Mrs. Wickersley, no one is advocating the mixture of races here!"

"No?"

"Of course not! These two people aren't going to marry each other."

"And you feel that their reticence to do so actually improves the situation? As it is, we are lending legal acceptance to mere cohabitation. Cohabitation between races."

Nina leaned forward and asked:

"So what do you want Frank and me to do, Adelia? The decision has already been made. Penelope has moved into Mr. Cousins' house."

"We merely wish—"

Frank:

"And who is *we*?"

"A sizeable portion of the good people of Bay St. Lucy."

"I see. And these people's wishes are?"

"For you and Nina to reconsider your decision. Then, upon doing so, talk seriously with young Ms. Royale, as well as with Mr. Cousins. Nothing has been done yet that cannot be undone. And surely you see that your home here would be a much more appropriate home for the young woman than the one in which she now finds herself. Also I must point out—"

Silence in the room for a time.

Then Adelia pointed out the thing that she had to point out.

"Many of the people I'm talking about, the ones who are so concerned with this situation and your part in it—are members of the school board. It's important for them to believe fervently that our young teachers represent the deeply held and traditional values of the community."

Or they'll fire me, thought Nina.

Who finally stood up and thought about saying:

Adelia, we'd love to help you out here but right now Frank and I have to go over to the Royale's place and pick up a million and a half dollars' worth of heroin, then bring it back here and give it to some international drug dealers so they won't murder us.

But she actually said:

"Adelia, we'll think about what you've said here. We really will. We do have a rather pressing errand to run now, so—"

"Of course!"

The woman rose and walked toward the door.

"Young marrieds, much to do, even this early in the morning! I do apologize for disturbing you at this hour. It's just that in view of circumstances—well, I hardly know how to put this without it sounding wrong—"

"Go ahead and say it. We understand that you have only Penelope's welfare at heart."

"There are people in town of lower mentality, lower income, lower educational status—"

"And these people might do something violent?"

Adelia Wickersley put her hand on the door knob while shaking her head:

"I hardly think it would come to that. More likely, the worst that might happen is that there might be comments hurtful to both Ms. Royale and Mr. Cousins."

"That would be unfortunate," said Frank, moving toward the doorway himself, so as to create air currents sufficient to push Adelia Wickersley out of it.

"It certainly would. The bottom line then all around is that if the two of you could with all due haste make everyone involved in this matter reconsider their positions—"

"We'll do what we can."

"Thank you so much. Have a good day then."

"Good bye, Adelia," said Nina.

And then the principal was gone.

And then the two of them were left, as they had been a few moments earlier, standing in the middle of the living room floor, staring at each other.

Finally Nina broke the silence by doing what she often did in situations similar to this, even though there had never before in her life been a situation quite like this.

She quoted Shakespeare:

"This is Hermia's line, Frank, from *A Midsummer Night's Dream*."

"And it goes?"

"I am amazed and know not what to say."

The clock on their wall kept ticking.

CHAPTER ELEVEN: AND THEN, SOME FINAL MATTERS TO ATTEND

By the time their Volkswagen pulled into the small driveway of the Royale's little pine-shingled house, only one police car sat before them.

"That's Moon Rivard behind the wheel," said Frank, turning off the ignition.

"And Trudy Parker is sitting in there beside him."

"What have you got there, Nina?"

"It's a little purse I use for traveling. They're not going to let us out of there with a bag of heroin in our hands, and I think they'll be suspicious of an attaché case too. But this—well, this looks like something we'd put a few of Penn's clothes in."

"That makes sense. Okay, let's go."

She got out of the car.

Together they walked toward the house, listening to rain spatter on their trench coats.

A siren could be heard from the direction of town.

Now two sirens.

"That's the forensics team," whispered Frank.

The driver's side window lowered on the police car as they approached it, and Moon Rivard's Cajun Prairie smile radiated out of it.

"Good morning, Mister Frank, Miss Nina! Hear about the storm that may be coming?"

"Good morning, yourself!" answered Frank. "Yeah, we're already drenched. Let's hope the thing goes north and misses us!"

The smile didn't go away; it was joined by a second one from the other side of the car:

"Nina!"

"Trudy!"

"Frank!"

"Trudy!"

And so now they had greeted themselves.

"Got a lot of folks coming over here, Frank."

"So I hear."

"The FBI is joining the party."

"My God. FBI in little old Bay St. Lucy."

"Yeh, I don't know. Apparently the folks in New Orleans think this might be a bigger matter than just one drug head overdosing his whore. Excuse my French, ladies."

Nina did not quite excuse it, but there were larger matters to attend to, so she said nothing.

Nothing except:

"Trudy, Frank and I have a bit of a problem, and we need to ask y'all a favor."

The second person plural *y'all* was always useful in the South when asking a favor.

Trudy leaned across the front seat and smiled:

"What can we do for you, Nina?"

"We need to get back into the house."

Silence for a time.

Then Moon:

"We're actually not supposed to let nobody in. Crime scene, you know. Now, with the FBI boys comin'—"

Think Nina think Nina think Nina—

"We only need a minute. I'm sure we'll be out before they get here. By that time we'll have driven away and they won't have the slightest idea we've been here at all."

Well, that wasn't much in the way of thinking, but it was all she'd been able to come up with.

Trudy:

"It's just that, well, it's very important not to touch anything."

Frank:

"We understand. The fact is, I've been involved in a good many cases where a home has been the scene of the crime. I've seen how things can go wrong, especially for the prosecution, if somebody goes inside before the police and runs around like a bull in a China shop—"

Moon:

"Yeh, they's being especially careful on this one. Damned if I understand it. They must think whoever killed her was in that house and left some fingerprints. Or something."

Right, thought Nina.

Or something.

"So anyway," she said to Trudy, "there are some things in there that the ladies missed last night when they helped Penn move."

Moon nodded, slowly:

"That was tough last night, tough all day for the young girl. And then, of course, what I had to tell her this morning, about her ma bein' murdered and all."

Silence for a time, the sirens still wailing in the distance, mixing with the sounds of an ocean half a mile away and gulls fifty yards overhead.

"How did she take it, Moon?" asked Frank.

"She took it well. She's a tough girl, a strong girl. I don't know, I tell her, she nod, it almost like she was expecting it."

"Maybe in a way she was. Anyway, if you guys could let us in for just a minute—these things they forgot to get—"

"What was dey anyway, Frank? What's so important to Miss Royale this morning?"

Frank hesitated.

Nina did not.

"Her underwear," she heard herself saying.

"Her—"

Moon was speechless.

Trudy was not.

"Come on," she said to Nina.

And she got out of the car, then paced toward the house, shaking her head:

"I don't know exactly who was over here helping move this girl's things. But there had to be a man involved. Leave her underwear behind indeed!"

Nina followed, then Frank.

Moon was still in the car, shaking his head:

"Y'all don't touch nothing, you hear? And get out of there before those Feds come, and those other boys from Washington!"

"We will," said Frank.

And then they were in the house.

Everything was perfect. The light green carpet, the ivory cloth-covered couch, the drawn blinds, the chair in a corner, the ceiling fan not moving at all, the wastebaskets empty in two corners, the pictures of ocean scenes hanging on the walls—

—all perfect.

But if it was so perfect, why did Nina feel this sense of dread as she walked into and across the living room.

Why this sense of depression?

Then, of course, she knew.

The house wasn't perfect; it was dead.

"I think what I need," she said, quietly, "is back in one of these bedrooms."

She walked into the hallway, looking first to her left and then to her right.

The larger and darker bedroom was the one to the right.

Clearly the mother's room.

"Trudy," she said, lying through her teeth now, "I'm not sure which one of these rooms was Penn's. Could you look at this one on the left? I know you aren't supposed to touch anything, but if you could just use a tissue or something and open the vanity. I think Penn's things will be in a top drawer."

She could hear Trudy behind her:

"I think I can do at least that much, Nina. It doesn't seem likely to me that the secret behind this murder will be on the handle of the top drawer of a sixteen-year-old girl's vanity."

Nina, exhaling a sigh of relief, turned to the right.

The small plaid-cloth suitcase was clutched in her hand, which she held tight, protected like a newborn baby, against her chest.

She entered Eva Royale's bedroom.

Light filtered through the window, which had no curtain, and exposed a shaft of dust particles hanging in the air.

"Okay, this is it," she whispered to herself.

The closet door stood mute to her left.

She opened it.

A row of clothing, hung as neatly as might have been expected of a soldier on a military base.

The hooks on all the clothes hangers facing the same way.

There a print skirt, there a black evening dress, there a beige blouse.

Dead clothes in a dead closet in a dead house waiting for a dead woman lying in a morgue.

And above them, a foot taller than the level of Nina's eyes, the shelf.

Upon which lay folded neatly a blue sweater.

She reached up, lifted the sweater down, and tossed it beside her on the bed.

There, beneath it, sat the brown leather attache case, perhaps eighteen inches square and four inches deep.

As carefully as she could, she lifted it down and placed it on the bed beside the sweater.

"I don't see anything in this first drawer," Trudy said from the adjoining room, "except t-shirts."

Nina's voice was dry in her throat.

"Try the second one."

"All right."

And there it was, the case directly beneath her hands, its locks and hinges gold in the sunlight filtering through the window.

"Don't be locked," she whispered to the thing lying an inch below her hands.

She reached down and pressed simultaneously two yellow metal buttons.

Sprong! The fasteners leapt upright and stood an inch and a half tall in perfect drill-attention.

As carefully as possible, she lifted the brown leather cover and opened the case.

It was empty.

CHAPTER TWELVE: RECONSIDERING THE SITUATION

She stood stock still for a few seconds, having no idea at all what to do.

Then some reasoning ability returned to her mind. She replaced the empty attache case on the shelf where she'd found it, then grabbed the blue sweater and stuffed it into the plaid bag she'd brought with her.

"I found her things," she said, turning and walking into the hall.

Trudy followed.

"You have everything she needs?"

Nina nodded, catching Frank's eye as she did so. He was standing perfectly still in the middle of the living room.

There was nothing Nina could say to him, so she continued to speak over her shoulder to Trudy:

"I have all she'll be needing for now. There are other things that we'll pick up for her after the house has been searched. And we'll have to figure out what to do with Eva's dresses."

"Of course."

"Frank, we need to get out of here before the police show up. come on. Those sirens are getting louder."

She didn't look at him again, but merely walked outside, said something meaningless to Moon, whom she barely noticed, got into the passenger's side of the Volkswagen, and waited for Frank.

He was exiting the house now; now saying yet another meaningless thing to Moon; now crossing the driveway; now opening the door; now getting in, now starting the engine.

Small Volkswagen vroooom sound—

And now asking:

"Did you—"

She interrupted him.

"It was empty."

"What?"

"Back out. Let's get out of here."

He did.

They did.

A quarter mile later, they were sitting in the parking lot of some store or other, she had no idea which.

He had killed the engine and was sitting quite still, studying the steering wheel.

"It was what?"

"Empty."

"What have you got in the bag then?"

"A blue sweater."

"Not a million and a half dollars' worth of pure heroin?"

"No, a blue sweater."

"Was the attache case there?"

"Yes. Right where Johnson—"

"Or Smith or Brown or Pink."

"Whatever. Right where he said it would be."

"You opened it?"

She stared at him for a time, then said:

"No, Frank, I just drew a few pornographic stick figures on it with some chalk I happened to have with me at the time."

"Sorry."

"*Of course* I opened it. There was nothing in it."

"Did you look at the shelf?"

"The shelf was empty except for the case and the sweater. I put the case back. The sweater, like I say, is here in the bag."

"Well. At least we didn't make the trip for nothing."

"No. We have this sweater."

They sat for a time.

The store in front of them, whatever it sold, was deserted.

"What do we do, Frank? They'll be coming for the heroin. And soon."

"You don't think they'd settle for the sweater?"

"This isn't funny. These aren't the kind of people who play around."

"No. They're not."

"We can't go back home. They'll be there waiting. Maybe Johnson. But maybe the man who killed Eva. Or somebody like him."

Frank took a deep breath and said, quietly:

"You're right about all that. Which means there's only one thing we can do. And we have to do it now. And we should have done it earlier. We should have done it first thing, after we got back from New Orleans."

"What's that?"

"The police. We have to go to the police."

"And tell them what?"

"Everything. The truth. Exactly as it happened."

"You want to go back to that house and tell this story to Moon Rivard?"

He shook his head.

"We can do better than that."

"The FBI?"

"No. I don't know anybody in the FBI. Whoever's in that house now and going over it, they're all strangers to us."

"Who do we tell, then?"

He turned and looked at her, then said:

"Davis."

"The judge?"

"Yes. He may not be much, but he's the smartest man I know in Bay St. Lucy. And the police will do what he tells them to do."

"Protect us? And Penn?"

"Absolutely. Now let's go. It's late enough in the morning, even on Saturday, he'll almost certainly be in his office."

And so they drove off, heading to the same town hall where the previous evening—how many weeks months years ago that seemed now!—Penelope Royale's fate had been decided.

The town was well along now on its process of waking up on a Saturday morning. The rain had intensified, but that didn't matter. The blinds going up in store windows; the small parks gradually filling with children and parents; delivery trucks, their drivers straining to lift open their ponderous tailgates so that the foodstuffs, tools, pharmaceuticals, razor blades, bird feeders, cat callers, dog whistles, nail polish remover, and whatever else a community had to have in order to survive, could be dispensed accordingly. And the poem came back to Nina:

About suffering they were never wrong,
The old Masters: how well they understood
Its human position: how it takes place
While someone else is eating or opening a window
or just walking dully along;

It was true. There, over there, someone was eating. There, up there, someone was opening a window. And there, to their right, on the sidewalk, someone was walking dully along.

She looked behind them.

A gleaming white cruise ship seemed motionless, as though neither the ocean nor the horizon existed in reality, and all of Bay St. Lucy was being deceived by a tremendous oil painting of these things.

But no, no, as she watched, the ship did indeed move.

Making true the rest of the poem:

And the expensive delicate ship that must have seen
Something amazing, a boy (in this case girl) falling out of the sky,
Had somewhere to get to and sailed calmly on.

Five minutes later they were in Judge Davis' private chamber.

She remembered it so well from the previous evening; it was beginning to seem like her own living room.

The judge was attending to other matters. They were brought coffee, which they sipped while staring at the OBLIGATORYPALEGREENFORBUREAUCRAT wall on the far side of the room.

"Frank are you sure about this?"

"Yes, of course, I am. There's nothing else to do."

"You really think that they can protect us?"

"They are the police. It's their job to protect people."

"But these are professional assassins."

"They're also strangers. Anybody here who doesn't belong in Bay St. Lucy will stand out. After we tell Davis what's going on, do you think Johnson, or anybody remotely like him, is going to be able to go down to those docks and just go knock Penelope on the head? Or kidnap her?"

"Bay St. Lucy doesn't have that many policemen."

"No, but the FBI does."

"I guess that's true."

"No, trust me on this, Nina. It's almost certainly a bluff. They're not nearly as clever as they want us to think. They won't be able to get to us. And they'll certainly never be able to get to Penelope."

"All right, Frank. I believe you."

The door to the small chamber room opened and a brightly smiling young woman stuck her head in, saying:

"The judge will see you now."

"Thank you," said Frank.

"Oh God," whispered Nina, to herself.

For Judge Davis was indeed walking into his chambers—followed by Homer Baron Robinson.

And Penelope Royale.

"Frank! Nina! Wonderful coincidence that you decided to drop by this morning. Mr. Robinson only just arrived himself, bringing Miss Royale along."

"Yes," said Frank, weakly. "So we see."

"Mr. Robinson—along with his wife and family— have a proposal to make. He wanted to come by and make it officially in my presence."

"Mr. Robinson came by the boat about half an hour ago," said Penelope, who was clad in a floppy gray sweatshirt and faded blue jeans. "He told me that he had some ideas about my future, and would I mind to come with him here to the judge's office. I was kind of busy—Lazarus is teaching me how to use bait, and how to kill sharks. But Mr. Robinson was so nice, I couldn't hardly say no."

No you couldn't, Nina found herself thinking. No, girl, you couldn't say no. Not to Mr. Robinson.

Whom Nina was seeing close up for the first time.

The first thing that struck her about him was his suit. She, a child of Bay St. Lucy, had never seen a real suit before. True, she'd seen the black and gray and sometimes navy blue or even white fake suits worn by local ministers and undertakers. Frank himself had a number of such fake suits, which he was forced to go to work in, and to court. But these things, she now realized were not *suits,* any more than the child's play ribbons hanging not infrequently about the neck of her professional male acquaintances were *ties*.

No, the absolute coal black garment that had been fitted like a movie set around this man standing before her could have stood perfectly erect without a flesh and blood human being inside it. Not that it was inflexible, for it seemed so soft even from a ten-foot distance that she wanted to reach out and pet it—but more that it had a soul about it, a statement that its very existence made, and that said "No" to wrinkles, unseemly creases, ill-fitting seams (*Nay, madame*, she found herself thinking, *this suit knows not seams*) and any being that did not have lots and lots and lots of money.

The man inside the suit smiled.

His red silk tie smiled with him.

So did his sleeves, lapels, pants legs, belt, and polished-like-glass shoes.

"Miss Royale was nice enough to stop her work and come with me. It was a gracious gesture on her part, since she'd never met me before. As far as she knew, I could've been kidnapping her to be sold into slave trade."

The room laughed.

So did Penn.

Nina and Frank did not.

"I'd seen you around," said Penn. "I knew who you were."

Oh really, Nina found herself thinking. *You really knew who he was?*

Okay, then you may be the only one on the face of the earth who did.

No, Penn did not know him.

Nor did Nina.

But she could not stop looking at him.

His hair, black as his suit and slicked back, was not *receding*, although it might have been termed so had it been found lying on the scalp of other men. This hair was *awaiting*. It was perfectly positioned, and for all its ten thousand soldiers (hairs to others, troops to this man) there would be not one instance of disarray, nor would a comb ever be needed to reform the ranks.

Homer Robinson was slightly taller than the judge who stood beside him, but he would be slightly taller than anyone who stood beside him. His skin was vampire-white, flour-basted white, never been in the sun white, Moby Dick whiteness of the whale white, that contrasted elementally with everything else about him—suit shoes belt hair and, most of all, eyes—which were as black as that part of the universe where no light is ever allowed to come, and which hardly can be said to be a part of our universe anyway.

It was strange, Nina found herself thinking, the effect of this near-albino whiteness. It was unnatural but not weak. It did not hint of sickness; it hinted at other-creatureness. And, in fact, there was something about the movements of this man, even in the few steps he took walking into the chamber, that seemed reptilian. His hands did not extend and then bend backwards; they struck and recoiled.

And the deep voice, the mellow baritone that was a coffee cream voice, a mixture of his absolute blackness and absolute whiteness that produced a pure caramel tone—somehow, was there not a constant hissing in it?

"Let's all," Davis was saying, "sit down around the table. Miss Royale, we'll put you here; Mr. Robinson by her—"

"Thank you, Your Honor."

"Oh, it's Tom, for heavens sakes!"

"All right, Tom," said Homer Robinson, seating himself.

"You Bannisters can keep your places there—more coffee for either of you?"

They both declined.

Nina attempted to remain expressionless. She had no idea whether she succeeded.

Homer Robinson had Penelope.

Twenty minutes ago they'd failed to find the heroin.

Ten minutes ago they'd decided to go to the police, in the person of Judge Davis..

And at precisely the time they were to begin taking their only option, Penelope appeared, kidnapped.

She simply did not realize that she'd been kidnapped.

"Now, Homer," Richardson was saying. "Please tell us your proposal."

"Of course. Actually the proposal comes from my wife Evelyn. And from my children, Arthur and Emily."

Like hell it does, thought Nina.

It's ten in the morning? Evelyn, Arthur, and Emily are probably in sealed caskets lying down in the family vault.

"We'd simply like to suggest that Penelope come and live with us."

The judge nodded. Robinson continued:

"I didn't tell you of this proposal when I picked you up at the boat launch, Penelope, because I wanted you to hear it in front of everyone else."

Penelope nodded and said:

"It's a very nice offer, sir. It's just—I think I'm happy with Mr. Cousins."

"Well, he's a very capable man, I'm told."

"I want to learn the fishing business. It's like I told you all a few minutes ago. He's telling me everything about bait, and how to kill sharks."

Everyone smiled at this.

The judge leaned forward and said:

"Penelope, you should consider this offer carefully. The Robinsons, as I'm sure you know, are quite well to do. They could send you to college. To a very fine college actually."

Homer Robinson smiled:

"I have friends on the acceptance committee at Harvard. Both of them owe me a favor."

Penelope shook her head and said:

"It's just—I don't want to go to Harvard. I want to be a fishing boat captain. I knew it the first time Mrs. Bannister introduced me to Lazarus, and I got my first redfish bite."

"Well," said the judge, shrugging. "We did make a decision last night. You're still happy about it, Penelope?"

"Yes, I am."

"I must tell you, there's some talk around town about the fact that your living with an older black man is somewhat inappropriate."

Wait until you watch the Channel Five News, thought Nina. Or until you get a load of Adelia Wickersley's *good people of Mississippi.*

Penn leaned forward, anxiously:

"You're not going to make me leave Lazarus' house are you, Your Honor?"

David thought for a time, then his expression softened.

"No," he said. "We knew last night that there might be some talk. But as far as I'm concerned, you're still living with the best and most honorable man in Mississippi. Go on doing so, at least as far as the Court is concerned."

Penn beamed.

"Thank you, your honor!"

Homer Robinson, smiling, getting to his feet:

"Well, at least we tried. And I'm sorry, young lady, for disturbing your morning's work. If you want to come with me now, I can take you back to your boat. To bait and sharks lessons."

"Yes, please, and thank you again."

"You're completely welcome."

"Well, then," said Davis, "Nina and Frank, I'm told you wanted to have an urgent meeting with me. Shall we have it now, after Homer and Penelope leave?"

Upon hearing these words, Homer Baron Robinson, standing precisely between the chamber door and the meeting table, gave a look to Frank.

And then to her.

It was a look she was never to forget.

And she remembered Gretchen's lines, upon seeing the devil.

What does he want?

He wants me.

Frank shook his head:

"No, your honor. I don't think we need the meeting now."

"Really?"

"We just wanted to make sure you were confident about Penn's situation. And clearly you are."

"I certainly am."

"Then we should go."

The four of them left the room.

While Penn was getting into the car that had brought her, Robinson said to both Frank and Nina:

"I'm told you both like to eat breakfast at the new Italian Bakery. Bagatelli's, I believe. I'm going to take Miss Royale back to her boat now. Why don't I meet you for breakfast in say, half an hour? It will be my treat."

"Sure," said Frank.

And that was that.

CHAPTER THIRTEEN: COLD COFFEE

Bagatelli's was, Nina found herself thinking, exactly as it had been since its opening a few months before. And this, in a time of bad things, was a good thing. The flour that covered Signor Bagatelli's apron was, she was almost certain, really flour and not heroin. The Bagatelli's—recently married, she'd heard, and probably no more than eighteen or nineteen years old—yelled and screamed at each other as they did every morning.

"A PRONO DESPICIANDOSE! MOLARE *DINUSIA* ASPETTO PIACINTO!"

Gibberish.

But they yelled at each other because they loved each other (Italians, Nina had heard, were like that) and not because they wished to murder each other.

Thirty-five minutes after the meeting with Judge Davis which didn't take place, the two Bannisters found themselves seated in the bakery, a narrow concrete and oyster shell walkway that had no name wandering along just a few feet from their table, and hard rain spattering on the plastic roof above them.

"I don't want this coffee," Nina said, staring at dark brown liquid in the china cup on the table before her.

Frank shook his head.

"I don't want mine, either. But we had to order something. Couldn't just sit out here and wait."

"Of course, that's what we're doing."

"Yes."

And they waited.

And they waited a bit more.

"If we'd stayed and met with Judge Richardson. If we'd told him everything we know—"

"Then Penelope would never have gotten back to the boat."

They were silent for a time.

The coffee grew colder.

She could think of nothing to say.

The bag of heroin was gone.

"Frank?"

"Yes?"

But she merely shook her head.

What could they do? Where could they go?

They could do nothing but wait.

Which they did.

Finally, Homer Baron Robinson arrived.

He seated himself at their table, took a sip of his own coffee, which was steaming, and nodded:

"It's difficult to make good coffee. Really good coffee. The French and Italians understand the process."

Another sip.

"I've been fortunate to spend time in Florence. You on the other hand—both of you—are fortunate to be alive."

There was nothing to say to that.

"What possessed you to be so stupid? I had to use all my powers of persuasion. Otherwise, someone other than myself would have gone to the boat to find Miss Royale. Then that same person or persons would have found a way to get to the two of you, police protection or not. It might not have been today, or even next week. But it would have happened. A million and a half dollar product has its price and that price is blood."

He shook his head, took another sip of coffee and repeated:

"What possessed you to be so stupid?"

Nina had been on the verge of tears since their arrival at the bakery. Now her voice shook as she leaned forward on the rickety table and said:

"What do you mean by speaking to Frank and me like that? What have we ever done to you? Why are we even involved in this?"

He was deathly still for an instant, then nodded slowly.

"All right. You have spirit, Mrs. Bannister. That's a good thing."

"I'm so pleased that you're impressed."

Was that a smile?

No, almost certainly not. And if it had been, it was gone now.

And the caramel voice remained implacable.

"You were the best people I knew for the job. The only people, actually."

It was now Frank's turn to lean forward on the small table.

"Nina looked for the bag exactly where she was told to look. It wasn't there."

"Evidently. Otherwise you would have taken it to your home, given it to the messenger, and been finished with this entire regrettable matter."

"So what do we do now? We didn't take the damned heroin. And we don't know where to look for it."

"Find it. After that, I cannot vouch for the safety of the girl."

"But she didn't do anything! Why would they hurt her?"

Abruptly, Robinson got up from the table, saying:

"For Biblical reasons."

"*Biblical*? What do you mean?"

"The sins of the fathers are vested upon the sons. Only in this case the applicable words are *mother* and *daughter*."

"Penn is going to have to suffer because her mother stole heroin?"

"No."

"Then what—"

"No, she will not have to suffer. It will be quick."

He turned, took two steps back toward the interior of the bakery, and said:

"I'll pay the bill inside."

And he was gone.

The two of them sat for a time.

"What do we do, Frank? What in God's name do we do?"

He shook his head and spoke quietly:

"You're right."

"What do you mean?"

"I mean that what we do now, we do in God's name."

"And that is?"

"We go to Eva Royale's funeral. And when we're there, we pray for her. And for her daughter. And for us."

They sat for a time longer, holding hands.

Then they went out together into the rain.

CHAPTER FOURTEEN: BLEST BE THE TIE THAT BINDS

The First United Methodist Church of Bay St. Lucy was a relatively small red brick building with a white steeple and fifteen rows of pews. There were four large windows on each side of the nave, half of them made of stained glass and depicting scenes from the New Testament, the others clear glass, until more offering money came in to repair them.

There were perhaps twenty people in attendance at the funeral.

The Reddingtons, the Richardsons, a few members of the town council.

Not Adelia Wickersley, nor any of her friends.

The open casket, gleaming silver with onyx handles, lay just in front of the pulpit.

The minister greeted the congregation with consoling tones and expected words. He spoke directly then to Penelope, who sat black-dressed in the front pew, her gaze directed at the body of her mother lying in state directly before her.

After a time, they were all standing, singing along with the piano, none of them needing songbooks.

Blest be the tie that binds
Our hearts in Christian love
The fellowship of kindred minds
Is like to that above

Then came the brief eulogy, the praise of Eva as a single mother, a woman who'd suffered long and sacrificed much. The certainty of ultimate reward, the consolation of having brought to life and left behind a loving daughter who would be of great value to the community.

"Now, finally, you may pass by and view the body. Any who wish to kneel at the altar and pray may of course do so. Also, there are collection plates, meant for any monies that will be used to help the expenses of the Royales, and especially young Penelope."

The Bannisters were the last to go down.

Nina put an arm on Penn's shoulder as she passed the girl. She walked slowly by the body of Eva, who seemed more at rest in death than she could ever have been in life.

And finally she knelt by Frank, who had just put money in the shallow yellow plate with green bottom.

She paused for a moment and then prayed, saying:

"Oh dearest Lord Jesus, please let—"

But she was interrupted by the sound of the door opening in the back of the church.

Heavy footsteps entering.

Then a collective gasp from the crowd.

She turned her upper body to look.

Three figures were striding down the aisle, which was just wide enough to accommodate them abreast.

"Oh my God," she whispered.

Each figure was masked; each wore a floor length white robe with a flaming red cross printed on the chest; and atop the head of each was a conical hat, shooting at least a foot and a half into the air.

When the figures reached the altar, they were no more than a foot from Nina.

They did not view the body.

The center of the three reached inside his robe, withdrew a check, and laid it in the same offering platter in which Frank had placed his few dollar bills.

Then the one nearest Nina made a similar gesture, pulling out a small slip of paper and placing it directly in front of her.

The figures then turned and left.

The check, she could see, was made out to The Pathfinder School, in the amount of ten thousand dollars.

On the sheet of paper was drawn, crudely, the figure of a black man hanging by a rope from a tree, lynched.

CHAPTER FIFTEEN: A MIND LIVELY

The service ended quickly thereafter.

Penelope was engulfed by the Reddingtons and the Richardsons, who led her up the aisle and away from the coffin.

Frank, Nina, and Reverend Jacobs were left standing at the altar.

For a time, there was nothing to say.

Finally the minister, shaking his head:

"This is shocking. I've never seen anything like that. Not in this church. Not anywhere in Bay St. Lucy."

Frank bent, took the check from the collection plate, and held it toward the minister, saying:

"They left this."

"Yes. I saw."

Nina held out the crude drawing.

"They left this, too."

"Oh, my God. Did Penelope see it?"

"No. I don't think so. She saw those three monsters, though. She couldn't help but see them. Do you think they're still around?"

Frank shook his head:

"They aren't still around. It's daylight. They don't like the light. They prefer the dark, when they can dance around some bonfire. What should be done about this check?"

The minister shook his head:

"It's ten thousand dollars. They mean for it to pay Miss Royale's tuition at the private school."

"Yes, that's what they mean. I don't think anyone will be able to cash it, though."

"Why not, Frank?"

"Because it's all torn up," he said, shredding the check and hurling the pieces on the red carpet.

"You think that's wise?"

"Yes. So is this," he said, taking the drawing from Nina and ripping it in the same way. "We need to sweep this up. It isn't right to have dirty things at the holy altar of a church. Come on, Nina, let's go to the cemetery. I assume we'll see you out there, Reverend."

"Of course."

Arm in arm, they made their way up the aisle.

By the time they reached the door of the church, the crowd had dispersed, and people were getting in their cars.

The rain fell harder, and the wind was intensifying.

They were the last of six cars in the funeral procession. The town had become dark, gray, and glistening in the rain. Street lamps came on. It was all glowing and indistinct, Nina told herself, as though part of a kingdom beneath the sea.

They drove on.

Eva Royale's grave had been dug in a plot near the southeast corner of the cemetery. As they approached and parked, they could see a police car sitting nearby.

The mourners flocked like wet crows to the grave, and were soon huddled beneath the green tent that said Edgarton Funeral Home on its wind-whipped fringe.

Several men in trench coats were now opening the back of the hearse, pulling out the coffin.

Moon Rivard approached Nina and Frank.:

"They say a hurricane's coming. In Cuba now. May hit Florida. We'll get rain though."

Silence for a time.

"I heard," he said, softly, "about what happened at the funeral. I'm sorry."

"It's not your fault," said Frank, just loud enough to be heard above a plashing of raindrops on the leaves surrounding them.

"A church is no place for that bunch."

"They think it is. They see themselves as agents of God. Always have."

"Still, the police should never have let it happen. That's our fault. Interrupting a holy funeral like that. It's our fault."

"What would you have done, Moon? They didn't break any laws. It's not crime to wear white robes. Not a crime to put a check in the collection plate."

Nina stepped forward, shaking her head:

"It *is* a crime though, to threaten to lynch a man."

Moon:

"They did that?"

"Yes."

"In writing?"

"They made a drawing."

"You have it?"

"Frank tore it up. Along with a check."

"You tore up a check, Mr. Bannister?"

"I did."

"For how much?"

"Ten thousand dollars."

Moon was silent for a time, then said quietly:

"Good for you."

The coffin was in place over the grave now, Penelope standing by with a handful of soil.

The minister nodded at her, then said:

"Ashes to ashes, dust to dust."

She opened her hand and dropped the soil into the grave.

Then the coffin was lowered.

The crowd dispersed.

The rain was getting heavier.

Finally they were alone at the gravesite, and could see a van from the funeral home approaching to fill in the grave.

"All right."

By the time they had reached the car, Nina had begun crying.

She cried uncontrollably, her shoulders pitched forward, her forehead pressed against her knees.

Frank's hand was held against the top of her head, and she could remember thinking how warm his palm was, and how that palm was the only thing warm in a cold wet world that was devoid of light and heat.

It took them five minutes to get home.

By the time she'd reached her own living room, and was walking toward her own couch, the crying had lessened somewhat. Not because her grief had lessened, but simply because the current supply of tears had been used up.

Frank stepped in front of her before she reached the couch. He held her tightly, pressing her face against his chest.

Ah. There were the tears again, this time wetting his shirt as she continued to sob.

And finally she could hear him talking, just above a whisper:

"Nina, I'm so sorry."

She tried to answer but could not.

He continued:

"You were right before. This is all my fault."

She shook her head and was able to choke out:

"No, it isn't."

"You're the most wonderful woman in the world, and I love you more than life itself. And now I've gotten you into this—this horrible situation. You told me not to get involved with Robinson in the land closing deal, and I didn't listen. Now our lives are being threatened by drug runners. And at the town meeting, I told them we didn't want Penelope. I just thought it was the right thing to do, to let her go where she wanted to go. Sending her to stay with Lazarus Cousins seemed to me the most moral and upright thing in the world. Racism? I remember thinking. 'Why, this is Mississippi in 1969! How could there be racism here?"

And somehow, somehow, it happened again.

As it always did, when she was around Frank.

Entering that darkened part of her mind where rain was falling and coffins were being lowered into the ground, and people were hating and threatening and shooting and beating each other—entering even *that* part of her awareness, was, courtesy of her husband and lover and complete life—a small spark that spread and glowed and ultimately became—

—laughter.

It mixed with sobbing, and, after a battle of some moments with her facial muscles, it won and came out as—

—a smile.

She pushed back from his chest a few inches, looked up, and let him see it.

He had one, too.

Five minutes later, they were sitting in the kitchen, a pot of coffee on the stove, steaming cups in each of their hands.

"So the situation," said Nina, "is that the Ku Klux Klan is going to lynch Lazarus Cousins unless Penelope Royale moves out of his house—"

"—which she won't do."

"Which she won't do. But it doesn't really matter because a ring of international dope smugglers is going to kill her—"

"And probably him, too. And maybe us."

"And probably him, too, and maybe us, as an act of revenge because her mother stole a million and a half dollars' worth of pure heroin—"

"—which is now missing, and which nobody can find."

"The situation is further complicated by the fact that you and I can't go to the police because we're being watched every minute by who knows how many people, but at least by Homer Baron Robinson, who's a big time gangster."

Nina took a sip from her coffee, then said:

"That about it?"

He nodded and answered:

"Think so."

"Okay then. I think, Frank, there's only one thing to do."

"And that is?"

"I want to go to bed."

He put his cup down and looked at her:

"You want to what?"

"You heard me. I want to go to bed."

"What is this, some kind of last rites love ritual? The world is falling apart, everybody's about to be killed in ways so horrible we can't imagine it, and you want to have sex?"

She shook her head:

"I didn't say I wanted to have sex."

"So what then, foreplay?"

"I didn't know you knew that word."

"I read."

"No, Frank. Not sex, not foreplay. I just want to go to bed."

"I'm still not—"

"Without you, darling."

He looked at her, then said:

"Well, that takes the fun out of it."

She reached across the table and took his hand:

"I need to think, Frank. I don't know, it's hard to explain, but ever since I was a little girl, when things would go very difficult for me, I would find a book to go into, and suddenly I wouldn't be alone."

"You're not alone now."

She smiled and tightened the grip on his hand, interlacing their fingers.

"I know. And I love you so much, Frank. All of those things you were saying about it being your fault? None of them are true. You agreed to work with Robinson because of us, because we needed a house to raise our children in. And you persuaded the judge to let Cousins have legal custody of Penelope because he was the best man we have in Bay St. Lucy. And because there damned well shouldn't be racism in Bay St. Lucy in 1969."

"Except there probably is."

"Ya think?"

"Just a little, maybe."

"Ya think?"

"Okay, okay, but why does this mean you want to go to bed without me?"

"Because I want to go to bed with someone else."

"Do I know him?"

"It's a her."

"You're a lesbian?"

"She's dead."

"You're a necrophialesbian?"

"She's in a book."

"I've run out of terms."

"Then go for a walk. Go down to the beach and look at the ocean."

"The last time the two of us did that, we got kidnapped, you know."

"I think I can remember it. But Frank, I'm not kidding about this. There has to be a way out."

"Sure. Find the bag of heroin. But how? Nina, from the time Bay St Lucy learned about Eva Royale's death, people could have been going in and out of that house."

"You think someone from Bay St. Lucy took it? The Reddingtons or the Richardsons are now shipping drugs out of Marseilles? You think the Bagatellis are using it on croissants?"

Frank shook his head, then said:

"Nina, the truth of this is simple, when you think about it."

"Oh, really?"

"Sure. The guy who killed Eva learned where the stuff was, didn't he?"

"Yes."

"As soon as he did that, he got in touch with an accomplice, who, without Johnson or anybody else in the ring knowing, just went and got the bag of heroin. Before we got back from New Orleans, and before the cops made their search. Basically these two guys—or maybe more, I don't know—were just doing what Eva had been trying to do. And, they're pulling it off. Hell, they might be halfway around the world by now. And the heroin too. If it hasn't already been sold and turned into cash."

"That's persuasive, Frank. It's really very persuasive."

"Thank you. Now the big question is how—"

"Except it's wrong."

He looked at her.

"How do you know it's wrong?"

"Because I'm an English teacher."

"Well, I guess that would explain it."

"I'm an English teacher, and you're a lawyer. It's like Thomas Jefferson said."

"Great guy to be quoting now. Okay, what did he say?"

"We study war; so that our children can study law; so that their children can study literature. Now get out of here and let me do what Thomas Jefferson made it possible for me to do."

He looked at her, shook his head, and said:

"All right. Good luck."

And then he left.

She lingered for a time at the door to the bedroom, then went inside.

Books here, books there. All of her books, that she loved so much; and there, tossed carelessly on a chair in the corner, the copy of *Treasure Island* that Penelope had checked out from the high school library.

She moved toward the bed, wondering:

How could she explain it to Frank, this feeling that being sucked inside a book was not escape but attack? This feeling that the ghosts breathing within the pages talked to her, helped her, made her see things anew.

She lay down.

There beside her was the small paperback she'd been reading hours before—hours? It seemed like days, lifetimes.

Emma by Jane Austen.

She'd never read it before, which was strange, because she loved *Pride and Prejudice*.

In so many ways, she *was* Jane Austen.

"All right, Jane. Talk to me."

It was lying open to page 134.

She picked it up and read the words:

"A mind lively and at ease can do with seeing nothing, and can see nothing that does not answer."

"What are you saying, Jane? What are you telling me?"

A mind lively and at ease. *Her* mind was lively, casting this way and that for answers. So was Frank's mind.

But both of their minds were lazy, seeing nothing that did not fit their preconceived notions. The world was this way and it was that way, and so be it. Of course, drug runners had taken the heroin. Frank had to be right. And the drugs were gone and they could never be—

And then Jane came again to talk with her, saying:

'Think, Nina, think. See the *whole* chessboard; remember *all* the details. Make a *new* pattern. Or rather reveal the old one that had always been there.

What conversations were important?

Don't allow yourself to *make do* with seeing nothing, Nina. Remember every word and try to see what was actually—

And then she saw it.

"Oh, my God," she whispered to herself.

"Oh, my God!"

What was he teaching her? And where were they—"

Oh, my God.

She jumped out of the bed and ran outside the front door.

"Frank!" she screamed.

He'd been able to go no more than a hundred yards down the road.

In a minute he was back.

She met him in front of the Volkswagen.

"Get in!" she said, still almost screaming.

"What's going on?"

"Get in and drive. I know where the heroin is! And I know where it's going to be!"

He stared open-mouthed for an instant. Then he started the car and asked:

"Where's it going to be?"

She nodded, tried to make her voice as normal as possible, then said:

"Treasure Island."

CHAPTER SIXTEEN: A MATTER OF TRUST

The rain was coming down in sheets when they reached the dock area. Pier lights twinkled here and there, but no human movement was to be seen, the boats having all been locked down and chained tightly to their moorings.

The Sea Turtle rocked precariously as they splashed their way toward it, and, for a second, Nina thought it might be deserted. Then she saw the door to the hold open slowly. A lamp emerged, and, with it, Lazarus Cousins.

"What are you doing down here?" he shouted.

Nina answered:

"We've got to come aboard!"

He shook his head:

"It's dangerous!"

"Let us come on board!"

He seemed to hesitate for a time, then waved the lantern in a rocking arc inward and said:

"All right. Just get out of sight!"

The made their way over the gangplank and followed him down into the hold.

Within a minute, they were in a small cabin area, lighted only by an oil lamp such as the one Cousins was carrying.

Penelope, clad now in her sweater and jeans, stood before them.

Cousins was now descending the stairs.

Once in the hold, his black trench coat dripping, he looked at them and said:

"I heard you had some visitors at the funeral."

Frank nodded:

"Yes. I'm sorry, Lazarus."

But Cousins only shook his head:

"It's okay. Don't bother me none. I been around that kind of trashy behavior all my life. They want trouble and come to me, I give 'em all they can handle."

Silence for a time, only the roaring of the rain on the deck above.

Ranged against the wall were three barrels that said *bait*. They were the same barrels Nina had used to bait lines two days earlier, when Penn had nearly landed the marlin.

"What do you want here, Mrs. Bannister?" asked Penelope.

Nina looked at her, then said:

"I want to bait a line."

Penelope then looked at Lazarus Cousins, who finally smiled grimly and said:

"You always were good at that, Nina."

"Yes. So which of these barrels is the best bait in?"

Penelope:

"The first one, Mrs. Bannister. That one right over there."

Nina walked to the first barrel and looked down.

The barrel was filled, as it frequently was, with shaved ice.

Lying on top of the ice was a bag of what looked like flour.

She picked it up and held it out in front of her.

"My God," whispered Frank.

"I should have put two and two together," said Nina. "Earlier on, you said Lazarus was going to take you out to Storm Island. He was teaching you how to use bait. And how to catch sharks."

"Lots of sharks around," said Lazarus. "All you can do with them is kill them."

"You're re-creating *Treasure Island*, Penn," said Nina.

The girl nodded:

"I told you. One day I'd be Jamie Hawkins. Well. We've got the treasure. A million and a half dollars worth of it. We've got the fort."

"Fort Massachusetts."

"Yes. And we've got the pirates."

Frank stepped forward and said, supplicating:

"What's the matter with the two of you! You've got the heroin!"

Penn nodded:

"I always knew where it was. I always guessed what my mother was doing. I may be ugly but I'm not stupid. That night when she didn't come home, I knew she was dead. I knew it before you told me at school, Mrs. Bannister. I knew she was murdered, too. So I took the bag. Because I knew they'd come for it."

Frank:

"They *will* come for it! So give it back!"

"No."

"What?"

"No, I won't give it back. They killed my mother."

"But they'll kill you, too, unless they get that bag back!"

Lazarus Cousins opened a chest on the other side of the hold.

He took out the twelve gauge shotgun Nina had seen him use to shoot the bigger sharks, the twelve footers.

"They plannin' to kill her anyway, Mr. Bannister. They sharks. And when sharks start swarming around and the water be all bloody—why, when that happens, either the sharks get you or you get the sharks."

"But—but if you're scared to give the bag back to the smugglers, then give it to the police and let them protect you!"

Cousins:

"Did they protect you, Mr. Bannister?"

Frank:

"How did you know about that?"

'Because if you'd told them about the stuff, then they'd have been here lookin' for it. They ain't never showed up. Somebody stopped you, that's for certain sure."

Silence. The sound of pier chains rocking and the hull of the boat slamming softly, with the come and go of the waves, against the dock.

Finally they could feel the boat rocking with what seemed a great weight.

"There's somebody up there," whispered Frank.

"Cousins nodded:

"'Course they is. The somebody who followed the two of you."

Nina caught her breath, then said softly:

"I'm sorry. I didn't think. Once I figured out that you had the drugs, I just thought—well, I didn't think. Of course, we'd have been followed."

But Penelope merely shook her head:

"They would've been here anyway, sooner or later. They know they don't have the heroin. The only other person who could have it is me. I'm just surprised that they waited this long. No, we've been expecting them. And we've got our plan. I'm just sorry, Mrs. Bannister, that the two of you had to be involved."

Frank spoke quietly:

'That was my fault, Penelope. I got greedy and went into business with the wrong man. I just didn't—"

He was interrupted by a booming voice from the deck above:

"Ahoy! Permission to come aboard and speak wi' ye!"

"That's Johnson," said Nina.

"Who?" asked Cousins.

Frank answered:

"A man who calls himself *Johnson*, although I'm certain that's not his real name. He's a man we met in New Orleans. He's apparently one of the ring leaders of this little group."

The thunderous voice echoed again, and again the boat rocked with gargantuan steps.

"I said *ahoy* down there! Where be your manners?"

Cousins, still holding the shotgun, walked halfway up the steps leading to the deck, then shouted:

"Come on down! But do it slow!"

Within a few seconds, Johnson was backing laboriously down the steps, which seemed almost ready to crumble with his weight.

And within half a minute more, he was seated against a far wall.

There was a lamp glowing on each side of him, its dim yellow light radiating from his tangled black hair, and from the silver cross resting on his chest.

He smiled, broadly.

"Nice craft, this!"

Cousins:

"Thank you. Glad you like her."

The huge head nodded:

"Oh I do, I do! And that means a good deal, let me tell ye! For I knows a thing or two about boats, I do."

"So what do you want here?"

"A drop of rum, if you've got it."

"No, we don't."

"Pity."

Penelope, who'd been both silent and motionless to this point, leaned forward on her chair and said, quietly:

"You killed my mother."

Johnson's smile disappeared, and Nina could see thick corded muscles stand out in his neck.

Then they relaxed, and he merely shook his head, growling:

"Nay lass, I did no such thing. Never in me life, have I killed a woman."

"Then you know who did."

"Aye. That I do."

"Is he with you?"

"Aye, that he is."

"Then you need to go find him. Tell him I mean to kill him."

A look of black anger, followed by another shake of the head.

"I'll tell him so such thing. It might upset him. And he's a scurvy dog when he gets his dander up, I can tell you that. As for your mother—well, child, I must tell you that she got herself involved in a bad business."

"She didn't deserve what happened to her."

"Nay, probably she didn't, you're right enough about that. But now, as to that business—"

Silence for a time, or as much silence as there could be, given the wheezing of Johnson's breath and the clattering of the boat hull against the moorings.

"—that business is, your mother took some property belonging to me and to my friends. We mean to have it back."

He scowled at Cousins, then growled:

"You've got it. Don't you?"

Cousins was completely still for several seconds.

Then he nodded, slowly, and said:

"We've got it."

Johnson's face lit up, and he laughed.

"Of course ye do! Of course ye do! Ye would have had to have it! The poor lady, Mrs. Royale, she wouldn't have lied, not given the conditions surrounding her demise. And the good Bannisters here, Nina and Frank, honorable souls that they are, they would never have taken it for themselves, would they? Now let's get to it, then. Where might it be, this *belonging* of ours?"

Penelope nodded to the bait bucket, into which Nina had only moments earlier replaced the heroin.

"It's in there."

Johnson rose with difficulty, made his way in two great steps to the bucket, peered down into it, and grinned:

"Why so it is, so it is! Look at the lovely bag a-lying there cold as the ice surrounding it, all mixed in the bucket with the mullet and the scrod! So then, now I'll just—"

Penelope withdrew from the pouch in front of her sweater, a black, glistening, pistol, and pointed it straight at Johnson's head, saying:

"We use this to kill sharks."

Johnson stared at it for a time, then smiled:

"Why, so ye do, I'll be betting. A forty-five that is. And good work it would do, too, with a shark. Blow him all to bits it would."

"Yeah. It's fun. Now go sit down and get away from our bait."

Johnson, chuckling, did as he was told.

When he had re-seated himself, he asked:

"Well then, where are we now?"

Cousins stepped forward.

He was holding his own shotgun parallel to the floor.

"I give up. Where are we?"

"Well, let's see then. Ye certainly have nothing to fear from me, for I'm unarmed. As for the rest of the men with me though—now that I can't say. As for their whereabouts—"

"They're in a yacht out in the harbor"

"Why so they are, so they are!"

"Saw it when it came in about an hour ago. You sailed yourselves down the Mississippi from New Orleans, then scrabbled along the coast until you came to Bay St. Lucy. Now you meanin' to take the heroin and sail for points east. Maybe Cuba, maybe the Caribbean."

"You're a perceptive man, Mr. Cousins."

"Thank you, Mister—Johnson, is it?"

The man sitting across from him dropped his head as though bowing.

"Johnson, of course. If that please ye."

"And why should we be studyin' to hand you this heroin?"

"Because we mean to kill ye, if ye don't. And there be enough of us to do the job."

"I could call the police now on this here two-way radio."

"And the four of ye would be dead before they got here."

Frank:

" And our alternative? A way that we may somehow get away from all this with our lives?"

"Why, the easiest thing in the world, it is! You simply give old John Johnson—or John Smith or John Brown or John Pink whichever one you please, for me first name truly is John and has been ever so long—"

"I know it's John," said Nina, quietly.

"What's that, Miss?"

"Nothing."

"She is," said Penelope, quietly, "an English teacher."

"Aye, of course she is, of course she is! But as I was about sayin': just give old obliging John that bag in that barrel there, and I'll get back on me rowboat, row back out to me yacht, and up anchor. Ye'll never see any of us again. Simply give us an hour, that's all we ask. Then ye go back to your homes, safe as church mice. And ye've got a nice tale to tell your grandchildren. Ye must act quick though, because word is there's a hurricane a brewing, and I don't like the look of the sea right now."

"The hurricane," said Cousins, quietly, "will swing north from where it is now, and hit Florida. We not gonna get no more rain than we be getting right now. It won't touch the Mississippi coast."

"And can ye' promise that?"

"I can for certain. Lived here all my life, always on the water."

"Good to hear, good to hear. And so. So. Ye should see the way clear, clear as that bell out on your mizzen mast."

Cousins nodded.

"Yeah, I see. You right you right.. And you give us your word. We give you the bag and you gonna' leave us and the Bannisters alone?"

"My word as an English gentleman."

"All right. Penn?"

She rose, saying:

"Yes, Lazarus?"

"Give him the bag."

"Are you sure?"

"Yeah we got no other choice in this here world. I saw myself seven of the devils on that deck when the yacht done pull into the harbor. May be more. We wouldn't have no chance. And the Bannisters wouldn't neither."

Penn took two deep breaths, then walked over to the bait bucket. She reached inside, took out the bag, and handed it to the man who on occasion called himself *Johnson*.

He took it, smiled, tucked it inside his sprawling white shirt and said, cheerfully:

"Thank ye, thank ye ever so much! Now this, this, is the way to do business. No noise, no blood. And so, I'll be bidding you adieu!"

He heaved himself out of the chair, and made his way over to the steps, which he climbed as laboriously as he'd descended them earlier.

Within a minute he was gone.

There was silence for a short time in the small cabin.

Nina finally broke it by saying:

"So, Lazarus, do you believe him?"

Lazarus smiled and shook his head:

"No. They gonna' be over in five minutes. They don't even have to come down here, they don't. Probably got assault rifles. Or they could heave a Molotov cocktail at us, blow up the boat. The police, the FBI—they'd never know for sure what happened."

Nina rose and made her way to Frank.

Within a minute, she was crying in his arms again.

"Oh, Frank, I love you so! I don't want to die. I don't want to die like this!"

But then she felt a hand on her shoulder.

It was Cousins' strong grip.

And it was accompanied by his soothing caramel voice, saying:

"Don't worry, Miss Nina. You know I wouldn't let nothin' happen to you."

She looked at him:

"But you just said—"

"I just said that he was lyin' through his damn teeth, and that his plan surely is to come back and kill us. They would have done it before, but they had to get the heroin. They blow up the boat, the heroin done gone."

"But now they've *got* the heroin! Penn just gave it to them!"

"That right?"

"I *saw* her give it to Johnson!"

"Or maybe you just thought you did."

"No, I'm not going crazy! He put it in his shirt!"

"Penn?"

"Yes, Lazarus?"

"Reach down into that third bait bucket, plumb to the bottom."

"Got it."

"Now show these here Bannisters what real bait looks like."

She burrowed in the bucket; Nina could hear the rattling of ice shards.

Then Penn straightened and held her hand out.

In it was a clear plastic packet containing white powder.

"What—what's that, Penelope?"

"Pure grade heroin. The heroin my mother stole."

"But what was the stuff you gave Johnson?"

"Flour. A bag of flour. I got it at Bagatelli's this morning."

The two Bannisters stood for a second, awestruck.

Lazarus spoke quietly to Penelope:

"Start up the engines, girl."

"Will do."

Nina:

"Where are we going?"

Penn, halfway up the stairs, turned:

"Storm Island. Fort Massachusetts. It's deserted now and off limits to park shipping because of storm warnings.

"But—won't they chase us?"

Cousins smiled:

"They gonna' chase us, sure, but ain't no way they catch us. I seen that boat and I know our engine. We faster. And by the way you two: sorry, but you gotta come with us. If we let you off now, well, there's too much of a danger that they'd see you from the yacht. Couldn't afford to leave you here."

"But," asked Nina, "what happens when we get there?"

"We do what you have to do with sharks. We kill them. Or we watch while something else kills them."

"What? What's going to kill them?"

"A sea monster."

"What are you talking about?"

"There's worse things in the ocean, Mrs. Bannister, than sharks. Huge things, that come up out of places deeper than where the devil live. One of those things is going to kill them pirates. And we gonna' watch while it happens."

"I don't understand. I just don't—"

"Don't you be worrying. Just believe in Penn and me. We know what we're about. We don't finish this now, we don't see them dead and gone forever—then we never get rid of them. This our best chance, maybe our last."

Within seconds, Nina heard the boat engine chug to life.

"You two hold onto something," said Lazarus Cousins. "Gonna' be one bumpy ride. Wind's at about fifty knots now, but sure to get stronger. Island lying twelve mile off shore surely take us an hour to get there."

"If we're faster than they are, can't we just outrun them? Lose them?"

He shook his head:

"I ain't studyin' to lose them; what I want is to *lure* them. We gonna' be the Judas goat to them."

"But when we get far enough away from shore, can't we just radio the Coast Guard?"

"No way the Coast Guard comes out in this weather. Too dangerous."

"Why is it too dangerous?"

"Cause of the hurricane."

"I thought you said the hurricane was going to miss us!"

"Big lie, lie that stink like dead fish stink... Hurricane's coming here, we be sailing straight as hell into it."

"But that's insane, Lazarus!"

"Maybe. But they running smack dab into it, too. Difference being, us here, we know what we doing. Radar in this old fishing boat, I know what thing is out there, and what thing is coming at us."

"All right. We trust you. There's just one more thing."

"What's that?"

"What's the name of this hurricane?"

Cousins shook his head.

"Don't know, they was just talking about it on ship to shore. Carol, or Katherine, or—oh, yeah, I remember now."

"So what is it?"

"Camille."

CHAPTER SEVENTEEN: THE TROPICAL DISTURBANCE

The origins of Hurricane Camille were from a tropical wave off the western coast of Africa on August 5, 1969. It tracked quickly westward along the 15th parallel north,[3] a tropical disturbance became clearly identifiable on satellite imagery on August 9. By that time, the thunderstorm activity concentrated into a circular area of convection. The next day, it moved through the Lesser Antilles, although there was no evidence of a closed circulation. On August 13, the wave passed near or over the southern coast of Jamaica as its convection spread northeastward through the Bahamas. Subsequently, it began a slower motion to the northwest. It is believed that a tropical depression formed shortly thereafter, early on August 14. On the morning of August 14, the Hurricane Hunters flew to investigate for a closed circulation near the Bahamas as well as near the Cayman Islands.[4] The crew observed a developing center in the western Caribbean, and winds had reached tropical storm status. It is estimated Tropical Storm Camille developed on the morning on August 14 with winds of 60 mph (97 km/h), about 50 miles (80 km) west-northwest of Grand Cayman.[4][5]

As the storm approached the western coast of Cuba, it began rapid deepening, reaching hurricane status and less than 12 hours later attained winds of 110 mph (180 km/h).

Initially, Hurricane Camille was forecast to turn northeastward toward the Florida panhandle. Instead, it continued northwestward and rapidly intensified. Its eye contracted to a diameter of less than eight miles (13 km), and strong rainbands developed around the entire hurricane.

After passing very near southeastern Louisiana, Hurricane Camille made landfall early on August 18 in Waveland, Mississippi.[6] Maximum wind speeds near the coastline were estimated to have been about 175 mph (282 km/h) with a pressure of 900 mbar (hPa; 26.58 inHg).[4]

Along Mississippi's entire shore and for some three to four blocks inland, the destruction was nearly complete. The worst hit areas were Clermont Harbor, Lakeshore, Waveland, Bay St. Louis, Pass Christian, Long Beach, and the beach front of Gulfport, Mississippi City, and Biloxi. One of Frank Lloyd Wright's waterfront houses for W. L. Fuller in Pass Christian, was completely destroyed.

CHAPTER EIGHTEEN: THE SEA MONSTER

For the next fifty minutes, Nina kept her forehead pressed against the glass of the small cabin porthole. She turned her head from time to time in order to smile weakly at Frank, who, on the other side of the room, was doing just as she was. She was trying desperately not to become seasick, and the fact that she didn't do so, she could attribute only to the fact that she was a seacoast girl and had spent much of her time in or on rough waves.

Although not as rough as these waves.

Nothing she'd ever experienced in her life was anything like these waves.

They were mountain waves, boarding house waves. The Sea Turtle climbed them at a 45-degree angle, then it dove perilously down again on water swirling beneath. Meanwhile, the wind was roaring so loud, that she'd have clapped her hands over her ears, had she not been using them to hold fast to the rails of the bench she was seated on.

Blue lightning—she'd never seen blue lightning before—seared the sky and illuminated the monstrous waves.

The rain was torrential, pounding now on the glass that she was attempting to look through, and blurring any distinction between sea and sky. It was all one, a murky dark gray/green, swelling and heaving.

At one point—she was not sure how long they'd been underway—Penn descended the stairs and leaned down to her, gripping her shoulder.

The girl had to shout as loud as possible.

"How are the two of you doing?"

Nina tried to smile, failed, tried again, and realized that the best she could do was make herself heard over the pounding rain, wind, and wave surges:

"We're surviving, kind of. How's the Sea Turtle doing?"

Penn nodded:

"Cousins is incredible. Winds are about eighty miles an hour right now, but he says as long as he keeps the bow pointed *straight into* the waves, we won't capsize."

"Penn—"

"Yes, ma'am?"

"Shouldn't we all be wearing life preservers?"

A shake of the head:

"We won't need them as long as the boat stays afloat."

"But what if it does capsize?"

"They won't do any good."

"Oh."

"Sorry."

"No, just—just thought I'd ask."

"That's all right."

"What about the pirates?"

"They're still chasing us. You can just make out their running lights. They took a couple of shots at us as we were leaving the harbor, but the waves were too big—I don't think the bullets came close."

"So what's our plan, Penn?"

"We'll reach the island in ten minutes or so. Then we've got to get up into the fort. And we've got to get into it before those guys behind us can land."

"Can we even walk in these winds?"

"Lazarus says we can make our way along, somehow, if the wind doesn't get above what it is now, which is still about eighty."

"And he thinks it won't get stronger than that?"

"It *will* get stronger than that. It'll get up to a hundred and fifty. But by the time it does, Lazarus says we'll be lashed down inside the fort."

"And what about it, the fort itself? Can it last through this storm?"

"You know that fort yourself, Mrs. Bannister. It's been here since 1860. Its walls are twenty feet high and five feet thick. According to Lazarus, its foundation bricks go down another twenty feet in the sand. It's been through Betsy, and through hurricanes before."

"Yes, but I haven't. At least not one like this. And not out in the ocean."

"Just hold on. We'll make it!"

"But when we do, Penn, what then? Those guys in the boat behind us are professionals. They'll have assault rifles, whatever those are. They might even have mortars, for all we know. They'll find a way to get into the fort. And they want that heroin. They're crazy to get it."

Penn tightened her grip and nodded, vigorously:

"That's why we've got an edge on them. They're not thinking. We are. At least Lazarus is."

"But what's his plan, Penn? Between the two of you, you have two guns—a shotgun and a forty five. As for them—we don't even know how many people are in that yacht. It's a small army that's chasing us."

"We'll make it."

"How? We're being chased by an army of vicious, well-armed dope smugglers, straight into the eye of a horrible hurricane!"

"Yes, and you forgot something."

"What could I have possibly forgotten?"

"The Ku Klux Klan wants to lynch us."

"Thank you for reminding me of that."

"It's all right. And, anyway, I don't think we'll find them when we get to the fort."

"What will we find when we get to the fort?"

Penelope shook her head, released her grip on Nina's shoulder, and rose, saying:

"We'll find the sea monster, Ms. Bannister. And so will they."

So saying, she walked up the stairs.

It took them ten more minutes to reach Storm Island.

She'd have had no way of realizing they were near the beach, for she could see nothing at all through the porthole now, not even the blue tracings of lightning that had phosphorized the churning ocean a short time before.

Her only way of recognizing their arrival was to feel a powerful lurch and hear the scraping of the hull on sand beneath.

A few seconds after this happened, both Cousins and Penelope were standing before her and Frank, distributing to each a section of thick rope and a black trench coat.

"All right," said Cousins, softly. "We heading out now. Penn?"

"Yes, sir?"

"Say good bye to *The Sea Turtle*, good ship that she was,"

The girl stood for a second, open mouthed.

"What?"

"*The Sea Turtle*. She gone."

"But—can't we just tie her to the dock?"

He shook his head.

"She might stay fast to the puny little landing dock now, with winds at eighty. But the big blowhard part of the storm is still out there to the East. Little over an hour and the winds are twice what they are now, maybe hundred and twenty, hundred and forty."

"The ropes won't hold?"

"No. Wouldn't matter if they did, because the pier will be gone."

"Are you saying," asked Frank, "that the winds here are going to be strong enough to blow the pier away?"

Cousins looked at him:

"No. I just saying the pier won't be here."

"But how—"

"Don't worry about it. She's a good old boat, and she got us out here through the bad edge of this whirlygirl. I gonna' miss this boat. Took my wife honeymooning on this boat. This *Sea Turtle*. I brought my daughter out, while she was still a little girl, and we were still—well, no matter. But what has to be, has to be. Now get into your rain gear. Take the ropes. Take one for me, too. I've got to carry this bullhorn. They'll be wanting to talk. Mr. Bannister, maybe you can carry this."

"What is it?"

"Ship to shore radio. Later on down the road we surely gonna' want to contact the Coast Guard, tell them where we are."

"Not now?"

"No, nothing they could do about it now."

"Can we," asked Nina, "take any supplies, any food?"

He shook his head:

"Be lucky to make the fort with just this much."

Frank:

"What are the ropes for?"

"You surely see when the time comes.. Now come on. That Fort used to be a hundred and fifty yards from water's edge. Monster tide now, though, and that distance probably down to no more than a hundred."

"Can we walk in this wind?"

"Think so. Wind coming straight out of the east, blowing over the fort. Means we'll be going straight into it. I'll go first, the rest of you follow single file. Penelope, you're strong as an ox. Anybody who falls, you pick up. There's one good thing about what we goin' into.."

"What?" asked Nina, shouting.

"Most people get hurt by high winds because they hit by something. Tree limbs, whatever. Or they get themselves electrocuted by fallen power lines. But—no trees on this island. Nothing to hit us. As for the fort, its electricity comes from some big generator inside the walls. So we oughta' be safe."

"Lazarus?"

"Yes, Nina?"

"How do we get into the fort? Surely it's locked down and deserted."

He smiled.

"You remember, we came out here the other day, I told you I'd run the ferry service?"

"Yes."

"I did some tour guiding, too. They gave me a key to one of the only outer doors that can be opened from the outside. I thought it might be smart to hold onto it. Never know what might happen. So I can get us in."

"What about the pirates?"

"They surely as all hell be landing in a few minutes at the pier, way over on the other side of the island. My bet is, they try to tie up their yacht. Foolish, but then they fools, no doubt about that."

"And then?"

"They come for us in the fort."

"Can they get in?"

He nodded.

"They got themselves enough firepower—AK 47's and such—they can shoot their way in, even though them gates is steel."

"Then what's to stop them from doing just that, Lazarus? Doing that and coming after us?"

"What's to stop them, Miss Nina, is that they ain't gonna have no time."

"I don't—"

"I know, hard to understand now. But you will later. Now, come on, let's get to that fort."

Getting to the fort was, Nina soon learned, only secondary to getting off *The Sea Turtle*, which had pitched hard to port upon ramming into the water-sand beach, and was now lying at a forty-five degree angle. She was able to totter up the stairs leading from the hold, but as soon as her head emerged from the solid walled cabin and became a target for the vicious winds, her balance disappeared and she could only grab for nothing or flail helplessly, while she felt her feet go out from under her and heard people shouting at her, their voices mixed with the roaring gale that was Hurricane Camille.

"Nina! Grab me!"

She had no idea who was calling her; she only knew that she'd fallen off the beached boat and was lying in six inches of seawater, her forehead bleeding.

Had she hit her head on the deck?

"Grab me!"

This was Frank, bending over her.

She took his hand and tried to stand.

She could not.

As strong as he was, and as hard as he pulled against her, the wind was stronger still, and so she remained motionless, rain pelting her black plastic trench coat, blood trickling into her left eye.

"Okay, I've got you! Just relax your legs!"

This was Penn's voice behind her.

Immediately thereafter, she could feel a vice-like grip around her ankles, just above her boot tops. Then her feet were pulled upwards and backwards. She felt weightless as a doll, and she realized she was being carried forward now.

"Grab my belt, Nina! I've got to turn around and face into this wind! Grab my belt!"

She did so, first with one free hand, then with the other.

And so their procession moved off, away from the beach itself, and toward the dark and monster-looming thing before them that she realized must be the fort.

"Just keep hanging onto Frank's belt, Mrs. Bannister! I've got your legs!"

How absurd she must look, she thought, being too weak to walk or even stand in the face of this horrid thing that was the storm wind, and so, carried like a rag doll, foot by foot forward, she was hanging parallel to the ground, and no more than two feet above it.

How was Frank able to keep standing, keep bending forward, keep walking toward the fort?

And how was Penelope, powerful as she was, able not only to walk into the wind, but to do so carrying the lower half of Nina's body?

She had no idea.

She had no real mental process going on at all, as she would learn weeks and even months later as she attempted to remember what this hundred yards stretch of howling/drowning/bleeding helplessness had been like.

She hadn't even sight to show her there was nothing but green-gray water-air to see, for she'd shut her eyes as tightly as possible.

She had only breathing.

That was the only thing she could do.

She could breathe.

She had no idea how long the ordeal continued, and she may have at one point have blacked out. She only knew that time, if it had stopped at one point, at least did resume again at another. This she knew, and her hands now around Frank's waist she knew and Penelope's grip loosened from her ankles she knew.

These things, and the massive walls of the fortress looming above her.

The iron door swinging open, its screeching, as well as what must have been a small rasp of metal against metal from the insertion of Cousins' key against the time-rusted lock—all obliterated by the winds screaming around brick towers and parapets.

And then they were inside.

She was still hugging Frank as tightly as she could.

"Thank you! Oh thank you, Frank! Thank you, Penn!"

They said nothing, but the three of them were tied in a human knot, laugh-sobbing, while Cousins stood no more than a yard away and said:

"We got to climb that circular staircase! We got to get to the top of this thing and out on the walls. *Now*!"

Nina could only shake her head and cry out:

"But we're out of the wind now! Let's just lock that door back and wait down here!"

"*No!*"

"But why not, Lazarus?"

"You all gonna' see that soon enough! Now come on—follow me!"

He heaved himself against the ponderous metal door, listened to the *click* as the locking mechanism engaged, then turned and walked fast across the inner courtyard of the fort, its red brick arches gazing impassively down at him.

The rest of them followed.

Nina dabbed at the cut on her forehead as they entered the narrow staircase that was to spiral around and lead them to the top of the walls.

As they neared the exit from the stairwell, she could hear herself screaming, at least mentally, if not actually:

Why do we have to go out in this storm again?

We at least had shelter down there on the floor of the fort. Why—

And then they were out in the wind again.

"Stay behind the bricks! They protect you from the wind!"

And that was true, she found herself realizing. They were walking on an earthen walkway, the same one she remembered transversing two months ago, when Lazarus had brought them out here. But immediately to her right, the brick walls extended up over the walkway by at least four feet. By bending down, she could get out of the wind. Peeping up over the wall, even though her face was torn by the gale, she could see the world extending out into the sea and beyond the fort.

And she could see the pirates.

Cousins had been right.

They'd tied their yacht to the wooden pier of Storm Island. Its running lights were still on, and, in a circle of light that must have been twenty feet in diameter, she could see them unloading boxes.

Finally, the four of them stopped walking and crouched side by side.

Cousins:

"See this metal rail at the base of the wall?"

She nodded, as did the rest.

"Okay, well, in about half an hour them winds up here sure to be a hundred and fifty miles an hour. By that time, we'll have to be tied onto the rail, or we get blown smack dab right off the walls."

"Why," said Frank, "can't we at least take shelter in the stairwell?"

"Can't do it!"

"Why not?"

"Cause—"

"Ahoy up there!"

This from a bullhorn down below.

Nina raised her head just above the wall.

Eight men were standing—somehow, she could not imagine how—in a line, halfway beneath the walls of the fort and the boat dock.

Two other men, somewhat closer to the boat, were opening the wooden boxes.

This done, they began distributing rifles.

"AK 47's," Cousins said. "Just what we thought."

"Ahoy up there! Aye, we know you're up there! Saw the tops of your heads as ye went creeping along."

Cousins produced his own yellow bull horn, the one that he'd brought up from *The Sea Turtle*.

He turned it on, stuck it just up above the wall and spoke into it.

His magnified voice shrilled out metallically into the wind:

"All right, we here! Now what?"

"It's a bad night out there, don't ye see that?"

"We got eyes, we see."

"Let's all go home. While we can. This little hurricane of yours that was going to go elsewhere— well, ye seem to have been a bit wrong about that."

"Sorry, made a mistake about that, I surely did."

"Aye, well it happens. It happens. The sea's a funny thing, she is."

"You right about that."

"So let's all get in out of the rain. Throw down the little bag of our product that we know ye've got up there with you, and don't be giving us no baking supplies now, as clever as that trick was."

"And if we do?"

"The same bargain we made before. We sail home, and get out of the rain."

"And then you let us go, all the four of us?"

"Why, of course, we let you go. Why do we want to waste ammunition on these thick iron gated doors? Now mind you, built for war as they was, we can still blast our way into them. It would just be so much easier, if we wasn't to have to."

"All right. Give us one minute. Let us talk."

"One minute it is. Have your pow wow."

Cousins turned off the bull horn.

The four of them sat together, rain driving hard on them now.

"Lazarus?" asked Penelope.

"Yes, girl."

"How long?"

He shook his head:

"I checked that radar just before we come off *The Sea Turtle*. Wasn't far away then—don't know, it should be any time now."

"What," asked Nina, "are you talking about?"

He took a deep breath.

"Both you, trust me. Everything gonna' be okay. Remember what I told you the other day when we were out here. These walls, twenty feet high. But the point on the island where the fort was built—where we're sitting—is ten feet above sea level. So right now we thirty feet above sea level."

"I still don't see…"

At that moment, Penelope raised her head slightly and said:

"I think I hear it!"

Lazarus nodded.

"Yeah!. It's coming!"

"Can I have the bullhorn?"

"Sure you can."

She took it, turned it on, and stood up.

"Penn get down," shouted Nina. "They've got guns! You're a clear target!"

But Penelope merely spoke into the bullhorn, saying:

"You killed my mother. Now I have only one thing to say to you."

Johnson took a step forward, smiled, and asked:

"And what might that thing be, my lass?"

"Turn around."

Nina could not help but raise her head above the wall.

Her back was to the distant shore and Bay St. Lucy.

She looked out into the ocean.

And saw the sea monster.

CHAPTER NINETEEN: THE   WORLD   HAS DISAPPEARED

For an instant she thought the blue lightning had returned, but then she realized the crackling purplish volts were all shooting through one wall of water, which, stretching from left to right as far as she could see, was racing toward the island.

"What *is* that thing?" she could hear Frank screaming.

And Cousins' reply, just audible over the wind and rain:

"Storm surge! Radar says it's twenty feet high!"

It was a blue-black wall of water, which seemed both to ride upon and swallow up simultaneously the flattened ocean beneath it. It sucked up lightning from the storm that had created it, and it transformed the electric current into vivid flashes which seemed to be boiling the smoking swell that preceded it.

It came at them with astonishing speed; she could hear its roar and watch it grow as it approached.

The men below had seen it at the same time: now they were screaming, though she couldn't hear them, but only see their gaping mouth movements and useless attempts to run.

For there was no place to run to.

Half of them turned and ran back to their yacht, but they reached it only in time to see the pier crumble and the boat thrown upon the shore, where it splintered, remnants of wood and metal carried then back into the sea as the waves were sucked back toward the mass of water approaching. The other half had run toward the fort, and had been stopped by its locked iron gates. Some of them had rifles. She could not see down to the base of the wall directly beneath where the four of them were huddled, but she could hear the sounds of faint popping as bullets ricocheted off metal.

She wondered for an instant how long it would take for them to shoot their way into the fort.

But these mental questions lasted *only* for an instant.

For the surge was at the beach now, consuming all land and everything else beneath it.

Now it was halfway to the wall.

Now it was striking the wall.

It did so with an astonishing shock, which made her think an earthquake had hit the fortress and that she would be thrown down off the wall.

"The rope, the rope!" she could hear someone scream.

Somehow she managed to loop the six-foot length of rope she'd been carrying around the metal rod that had been welded into the brick wall just at her feet. She gripped her hands around it and pulled with all her strength, her forehead now pressed hard against the bricks as water poured down on top of her, as though a huge vat of salt spray had been overturned.

Behind her and below, she saw the storm surge engulf the fort's interior. It did so with astonishing speed, so that in one second she was dimly able to make out the circular stairway they'd just climbed, and in another, she saw nothing but black, churning water, no more than fifteen feet below them, now ten feet, now five—

—and there it stopped, leveling out.

She could hear and feel the ocean, raging by only a few feet on the other side of the wall, tearing at the bricks.

"Hold on! Hold on!"

She had no idea whose voice was screaming.

The wind had increased now; thank God it was pushing her into the wall. She felt her ribs might give way because of the force of her body against the bricks, and the sea behind and just below her seemed to be trying to suck her back down into it.

But she held on.

She had no idea how long this lasted.

She could make out shapes to her left.

She knew them to be Frank, Penelope, and Cousins, but now in this unworldly mix of elements gone crazy, they were no more than indistinct forms.

Finally, the water began to recede slightly; behind and below her, she saw the top of the circular staircase, which had been submerged only seconds before.

She heard a voice, which she recognized as that of Cousins:

"The worst done past us now, and I'm bettin' the winds sure to be going down a little!"

The lightning changed now, flashing silver and illuminating both the sky above them and the waters around them.

She couldn't withstand the temptation to raise her head slightly, and peer over the wall.

The whole world was rain and water, water rushing like the torrents of a river.

The last of the surge, she found herself thinking.

And everything in its path had been obliterated.

The biblical flood; the earth itself and all its inhabitants gone.

Lazarus Cousins, although she couldn't hear him, was talking on the intercom radio that he'd brought from *The Sea Turtle*.

The Sea Turtle that was now no more, carried away as a mass of splinters by this creature that had almost subsumed and swallowed the four of them.

"Coast Guard! This is Cousins! We on the old fort!"

A rattle of static in reply.

"No. I know you can't. We can hold on. Surge didn't overtop the fort. Just get somebody out here soon as you can!"

She could now hear him shouting to the rest of them:

"They at least know we're here!"

Frank:

"Can they come for us?"

"No, not until the hurricane moves on and the winds start goin' down. We got ourselves a few more hours to be here. Everybody be sure you're tied tight onto that rod."

She found herself trying to scream as loud as possible.

She did so, and still could only hear what sounded like the voice of a frightened child:

"Lazarus?"

"Yes, Nina?"

"The pirates?"

"Gone. Ate up by the ocean."

Now Penn was talking:

"Lazarus, do you have the bag of heroin?"

"Yes. Right here."

"Please give it to me!"

"What you going to do with it?"

"There's only one thing to do with it."

"All right. Here."

Nina could see the girl rise, take the bag in her hand, and with one powerful swing of her arms, throw it out into the surging current.

As the bag disappeared, Penn said:

"I'm sorry, Mom. I know it killed you. It and those people. But it's dead now. And so are they."

No voices for a while.

Then Nina could hear herself again, asking Cousins:

"That horrible band of water—"

"Yes, Nina?"

"Bay St. Lucy?"

He didn't answer.

She could only see him shaking his head.

CHAPTER TWENTY: LANDFALL

Camille made landfall shortly before midnight in the Bay St. Louis area (USACE 1970). At this time, the eye of the storm was about 12 miles in diameter and crossed almost directly over the town of Waveland at a forward speed of 15 mph. The great volume of water moving inland up the Jourdan River floodplain was typical of other estuary streams along the coast. The volume flowing inland at the tide crest was estimated to have been at least 90,000 cfs. This volume is more than three times the flood discharge expected on the Jourdan River on the average of once in 50 years (Hudson, 1970).

Camille's intensity in Harrison County, Mississippi, was compounded by the geography of the area in which sections of the county were inundated from both the north and south (Leyden, 1985). Maps depicting the extent of flooding show that the community of Pass Christian and parts of Biloxi were completely inundated by flood waters. Storm waters rose to 22.6 feet at Pass Christian, 17 feet behind Pass Christian, 21.6 feet at Long Beach, 21 feet at Gulfport, 19.5 feet at Biloxi, and 15 feet on the Biloxi Bay (USACE, 1970) (Figure 4).

Although warnings were posted, there were a number of persons who were thought to be safe when they were not. A local minister's wife was swept to her death as tides destroyed the 100-year old church where she and her husband sought protection. Another woman climbed into the rafters of her mother's house along with 17 other adults and 13 children to escape the rising waters. The ladder on which they climbed was later used to pull two people to safety. Another family in a beachfront house sat in their downstairs living room watching the storm until water seeped in under the door. A mop, then towels, then a rug were used to try to stop the flow. The husband opened the door and was swept across the room by a surging wave. As the lower floor filled with water, the family retreated upstairs where adults gave instructions to children on where to go should they survive (Wilkinson & Ross, 1970).

Sea-going vessels and small craft alike were swept inland and deposited among the remnants of buildings. A large diesel fuel barge was lifted out of the harbor, carried ashore, and deposited on the medial strip between the east and west lanes of US Highway 90. Farther up on the beach, a large oil storage tank floated several miles from its original position (Rohlfs, 1969). Eyewitnesses reported that the storm surge remained ashore very briefly—only for some 20-30 minutes—sucking a large amount of debris back into the Gulf of Mexico with astonishing speed (ESSA, 1969a).

The strongest winds east of the eye struck between Pass Christian and Long Beach, Mississippi. Destruction in this area was almost complete. One survivor reported that she was invited by friends concerned for her safety to leave a safe location and move into an apartment building (Richelieu Apartments in Pass Christian). This apartment building occupied a low site formerly known as the *rice field*. It was destroyed and 21 lives were lost. A total of about 150 people died along the Gulf Coast during Camille's passage.

CHAPTER TWENTY ONE: HOMECOMING

By daybreak the sky had cleared.

The tides had receded, and the entire island was visible above the sea.

They had huddled on the walls for more than two hours, but after that, they'd been able to find shelter in the spiral staircase.

For an hour or more, Nina even slept.

She was awake though when sunlight began to pour through cracks in the brick walls.

And she was awake enough to differentiate the clacking of a helicopter rotor from the soft growling of the waves.

It was a large coast guard helicopter, bright yellow.

The two pilots helped them in, got their seatbelts fastened—then one of them said, shouting to make himself heard above the engine noise:

"We're taking most people to Hattiesburg! There's a rescue center there!"

But Nina, not waiting for the others to answer, shouted:

"We're from Bay St. Lucy!"

The pilot was silent for a time, then shook his head:

"Ma'am, you'd all be safer in Hattiesburg. They're building portable shelters there. People are being care-flighted in from all up and down the coast."

"No, no, we're from Bay St. Lucy! Take us home!"

Silence.

Just the chop-chopping of the rotors and the singing of an east wind.

"Nina—"

"Frank, tell him to take us home! I want to go home!"

"I think what he means to say is—"

But she was shouting again, into the ear of the pilot:

"Take us to Bay St. Lucy! Right now!"

"Ma'am—"

"What is it? What are you trying to tell me?"

"Ma'am, Bay St. Lucy is gone."

The four of them sat for a time, stunned, unable to speak for a time.

Then Frank, to the pilot:

"Are you ordered not to take us there?"

"Advised, sir."

"Is there a place to land?"

"Yes, sir. Helicopters are going in and out of the airport."

"So copters are taking people in there?"

"Well, sir—"

"Yes?"

"Mostly they're taking people out of there."

More silence.

The four of them looked at each other.

"I want," said Penelope, "to go home."

"I do, too," said Nina.

The pilots both nodded.

And the helicopter took off.

The flight back to what had been Bay St. Lucy lasted a little over fifteen minutes.

They flew over an ocean that resembled the ocean Nina had always loved. It was blue, as it always was, green, as it always was, topped by white, scudding foam, as it always was.

Then land was beneath them.

"Oh God!" she whispered, her breath clouding the small circular window of the helicopter.

The land some five hundred feet beneath them was like a game board of some kind, simply squares beside squares beside squares beside—

And then she realized what the squares were.

They were the concrete foundations of what had been buildings. Within these squares were various jagged shapes that had no pattern. These shapes were multicolored, and sometimes they overlapped the boundaries of the squares. Sometimes they were submerged by what seemed to be pools of glistening tidewater.

These shapes were the refuse that remained from the destroyed structures of the town.

Or they were remnants of cars, trucks—

—people.

There were no trees.

Nothing, she could tell, extended above the ground more than a few feet.

Below them and to their left, snaking between them and the small tracery where ocean lapped upon land, was a grotesque ribbon of huge concrete chunks, ripped out of the ground and scattered randomly upon it.

"That," she could hear Frank whispering, "was Breakers Boulevard."

Within two minutes the helicopter had landed.

They walked single file down the small metal ramp that descended from the helicopter.

Whatever was around them bore no resemblance to the airport, save for the shattered fuselages, wings, tails, and propellers littering the ground around them. There were no buildings. Merely refuse.

The heat was unbearable.

Helicopters hovered everywhere in the sky, some lifting off, some descending.

One of the pilots was standing in the copter doorway, pulling in the ramp.

"Do you have a place to go?" he asked them. "We can still take you to Hattiesburg."

Nina shook her head:

"No. This is our home. This is where we belong."

"All right. Good luck."

The helicopter took off.

And they were left alone among the chaos and debris that had been Bay St. Lucy.

Penelope, Nina could see, was crying.

Frank and Lazarus were simply turning in slow circles, their mouths open, fingers pressed against their foreheads.

They began to walk.

They had gone for perhaps one hundred yards in the direction of what had once been downtown, when they were overtaken by a police car.

They were still on the tarmac, which glistened with standing rainwater.

The air was filled with the sounds of helicopters landing and taking off, sirens coming and going, and people crying.

"Excuse me! Excuse me!"

A young policeman whom Nina had never before seen.

On his brown uniform shirt were stitched in gold the words "Pass Christian."

"Excuse me, I need to talk to you."

They stood watching him, watching the blinking blue light on the top of the car as it flashed and rotated.

Finally, Frank stepped forward and leaned toward the open window, then said:

"Yes? What is it?"

"Are you folks all right? Do you need medivac?"

They looked at each other.

Finally, Frank said into the window:

"I think we're all right."

"Ma'am," the officer said, looking at Nina, "you have a cut on your forehead. You need to get that looked at."

Nina stood mute, knowing nothing to say.

She reached up and gently touched her forehead. There was some dried blood, and she could feel that a scab had begun to form.

"I'm all right," she said, dully.

"Do the four of you have any place to go?"

"We're going home," said Nina.

"What is the address?"

Nina told him.

He merely shook his head.

"There's nothing there now. All those houses are gone."

Something seemed to stick in her throat. She could do nothing but shake her head.

Then she realized that Frank was holding her.

She sobbed for a time with her face buried in his chest.

The officer was still speaking, she realized.

"There are several buildings in town where they're taking people. A lot of the streets are gone, the concrete torn right out of the ground. Just big chunks of asphalt lying around like boulders. Not all the streets though. A few are still passable. Come on, get in. It's dangerous to walk because of the snakes."

Lazarus Cousins stepped forward and asked:

"Snakes?"

The young officer nodded:

"They're everywhere. Never seen so many snakes. The flooding must have forced them out of their burrows, or wherever they lived. Now they're just crawling around, or they're coiled up on the concrete squares that used to be foundations. They're mean, too. Strike at anything. Some of them are cottonmouths. No, it's too dangerous just to walk around. Come on, get in!"

They were about to do so when a second police vehicle pulled up, this one light blue.

Nina recognized the face of Moon Rivard sticking out of the window.

"The Bannisters! Lazarus Cousins! Miss Penelope! My God, I'm glad to see you!"

Frank stepped forward and took the hand that was sticking through the window.

"Moon! We're glad to see you, too!"

"We thought you were gone! Your house is—"

Frank stopped him:

"We know, Moon. We know."

"That wave came through about two a.m. Storm surge, they called it. We had some warning it was coming, and we were able to get a lot of people up onto roofs. Of course, a lot of folks had already left town, earlier in the night or late that afternoon. But after a while the winds had gotten so strong, and the flooding so bad—well, the roads were impassable. So we just did what we could."

Nina asked the question that the rest of them were too frightened to ask.

"How many people are dead, Moon?"

He simply shook his head:

"We don't know. A lot of people are missing. But we can't say yet. Everyone's just wandering around looking for lost kids, or wives, or husbands. We thought you four was dead. How did you get through it?"

Frank:

"Lazarus saved us."

"Good man, Lazarus. But it's a helluva good thing I found you. I been getting radio calls every minute for the last half hour or so."

"What calls," asked Lazarus, "and what they got to do with me?"

"Woman."

"Woman? I don't know no women!"

"You must know this one. She came in on one of the helicopters that are flying rescue people in from New Orleans."

"I still don't see—"

"She says she's your daughter."

Lazarus stood for a short time, completely still.

Nina could see that his eyes had begun to glisten.

"My daughter," he whispered.

"That's what she said. Lazarus, I didn't know you had a daughter."

"I didn't have. Not for what seems like a long time."

"Well, look, why don't you get in. You too, Miss Royale, since, from what I understand, Mr. Cousins is your legal guardian. Nina, maybe you and Frank can ride with this young man out of Pass Christian."

"Sure," said Frank.

The young officer looked at Moon.

"Where should I take them?"

"Take them to the Robinson place. That's where the biggest number of care units are."

Nina bent to get in the patrol car, and heard Frank asking:

"The Robinson mansion survived?"

"Yes. That, the court house, part of the Methodist Church. The bridge on highway 90 leading out of town is destroyed though. Crumpled up like it was made out of paper. As for the rest of the buildings, houses, trees—they're just gone, it wiped them out."

A bus pulled up, disgorged a group of people, then left.

The people all seemed to be wearing yellow trench coats, and were, Nina could soon tell, being herded to one of the larger helicopters that was sitting, rotors chopping, awaiting them.

Careflight out, Nina told herself.

One of the figures seemed to see the four of them, and then walk toward them.

Was that—

Oh, God, it was.

Adelia Wickersley.

She approached, looked beyond them out toward the sea, then stared at Nina and said, her voice quivering:

"It's all gone. All of it. The school, our houses. It's all gone."

Nina could think of little to say except:

"I know, Adelia. We all know.

"He's making us pay. We were living the wrong way. Black with white—it's as I told you yesterday. We were living in sin, and now he's sent the great flood to make us pay."

"I don't know, Adelia. It's a hurricane. Hurricanes happen."

But Adelia Wickersley merely shook her head:

"I'm going away now. My house is gone. All of our houses are gone. You should go too, Nina. Do not try to live here. There is a curse. Come. Kneel with me, the both of you."

She knelt down.

Nina, knowing little else to do to avoid a scene, knelt with her.

Adelia took a deep breath, closed her eyes tightly and said:

"Oh God—"

"What better can we do than prostrate fall

Before you reverent, and here confess
Humbly our faults, and pardon beg, with tears
Watering the ground, and with our sighs the air
Frequenting, sent from hearts contrite, in sign
Of sorrow unfeign'd, and humiliation meek.

Then she got up, said one more time:
"Leave, Nina. Leave and never come back."
She walked away, toward the medivac helicopter.
Frank, watching her, shook his head and said:
"She's crazy, Nina. But you always knew that."
"Yes. I guess she is."
"You guess? You think God sent a hurricane because Lazarus became the guardian of Penelope Royale?"
"No. No, Frank. But when I look around, I do want to water the ground with tears."
"I can understand that. But that work that she quoted. Do you know it?"
"I know it. All English teachers know it. And she was an English teacher."
"What was it?"
"John Milton wrote it. It's Adam to Eve, after he realizes the truth of what's happened to them."
"What's the name of the work?"
She looked out over what had been their home and said:
Paradise Lost

CHAPTER TWENTY-THREE: JOB OFFER

The Robinson mansion seemed to consist of two halves: the top half was much as it had always been, gabled and black-slate roofed, with small, lace-curtained windows looking out over the ocean, which glittered blue green in mid-morning August sunlight.

The lower half had clearly been under water. The glass had been blown from its windows. Weeds, dead and brown now, clung to the walls.

The grounds, where Nina and Frank had sat two months before, had been swept clean. No trees, no gazebos, no small white metal tables where plates of oysters might be served.

No, now there were simply ambulances, doctors, nurses, policemen, hastily erected huge green canvas tents—

—and people, people of Bay St. Lucy.

Old people, children.

People clad in hospital gowns.

People wandering, crying, hugging each other, waving their arms toward what had once been downtown.

She and Frank got out of the patrol car.

"If I was you," the driver was saying to Frank, "I'd get in line at one of the tents, maybe let the doctors check you out. The cut on the lady's forehead—"

"I know, we'll get it looked at."

"I've got to go now. They need me back at the airport."

"We understand."

They stood for a time, holding hands.

"Where do we go, Frank? What do we do? Where will we sleep tonight?"

"I don't know, honey."

"Maybe we can help out here. We're not medics, but we can comfort people."

"I don't know, I just can't—"

"If I can trouble the two of you?"

They looked around.

Standing behind them was the elderly African American man who'd announced two months earlier that Homer Baron Robinson was ready to see Frank.

He looked just as he'd looked then, with the same tuxedo.

And he was here to perform basically the same office.

"Mr. Robinson saw you arrive just then," he said. "He has been making inquiries about both of you. About your safety."

"Good of him," said Frank, sardonically.

"He has asked me if I would come and get you. He's waiting in his study."

"I don't think so," said Frank. "You can tell Mr. Robinson—"

"No," interrupted Nina.

Frank stared at her.

"What do you mean, *no*? You've told me for months I was crazy to get involved with that guy!"

"I don't know, Frank. I just have a feeling. And besides, if we hadn't gotten involved with him, we'd probably be dead now. Swept out to sea."

"I don't know, I just—"

But the man in front of them merely turned and said:

"If you would both just follow me—"

And they did.

The great house had become a hospital. They were taken from room to room, where people sat being bandaged, or lay with tubes in their arms, or merely huddled together on the great couches, crying or consoling.

The climbed a staircase, turned down a hall, made a second turn into another hall, and then followed their guide into a small darkened room.

There, behind a burnished oaken desk, sat Homer Baron Robinson.

He looked as if nothing had happened.

The same black suit, the same red tie.

He might have been sitting high in some board room in New York City.

"Please sit down, both of you."

They did so.

"I wanted to apologize for the ordeal you went through."

There was nothing to say to that, so they simply sat and waited, listening to the muffled sounds of sirens outside, and crying inside and below.

"Ms. Royale made a terrible mistake. It proved fatal for her and it could have been for her daughter. I thought the two of you might have been in a position to save the girl's life, and to do so with a minimum of pain, a minimum of effort."

"That's not the way it worked out," said Frank, quietly.

"No. But the girl is alive. As are both of you. You have my thanks for your efforts."

He sat quietly for a time, then continued, saying:

"I know that last night my—well, my *associates*— followed you to the harbor. I know that two boats disappeared out into the harbor. I assumed that you had been killed by them."

Frank:

"We weren't."

"And I'm extremely grateful for that. As for the *product* that was missing—"

"It's gone."

"I assumed that, too."

"That bag was—"

"Was lost at sea. Was taken by the storm."

"Yes."

"And exactly how it was lost, how it was taken—I don't care. I can tell you though, that I've spoken to certain other associates. Higher on the chain of command than the people you dealt with. I spoke with them last evening, and I spoke with them just now, after I saw that you were both safe."

"What did they have to say, these *associates*?"

"They are prepared to drop the problem. Pursuit of the product now seems likely to cost more in terms of money and effort than is worthwhile."

Frank leaned forward in his chair and said:

"So it's over?"

"It's over."

"For both of us, and for Penelope?"

"For all of you. A hurricane washed the problem away."

Silence for a time.

Then the tone of the man behind the desk seemed to change, and his gaze rested on some invisible object behind them.

"I need now," he said, "to discuss some other matters with you."

It was Nina who answered.

"All right. We're listening."

"My wife Evelyn," he said, "has left me."

And it was Nina who spoke again:

"I'm sorry," she said.

And meant it.

Robinson continued:

"She left last night."

"She'll be back, Mr. Robinson."

"No. She won't. She is probably happier where she is now. I had made her life difficult, and for some time. But I shall miss her very much, very deeply. Her wishes still remain important to me. And so I shall ask you, Mr. Bannister, to—"

The door opened suddenly.

Framed in it stood Lazarus Cousins.

Standing beside him was a tall and strikingly beautiful young woman.

"Mr. Cousins."

Lazarus nodded:

"I'm Lazarus Cousins."

"I know. I'm happy that you're well. I'd sent my people to find you. Obviously they succeeded."

"They did."

"I wanted to apologize to you. I think the apology should now extend to the young woman with you."

"My daughter."

"So I am told. At any rate. A disgusting spectacle took place at the funeral services for Ms. Royale."

"I'm told about it; I wasn't there."

"Good that you were not. Nevertheless it happened. But it will not happen again, Mr. Cousins. I abhor it. As did my wife. She always loved seeing the coming together of diverse cultures, diverse races."

Cousins nodded:

"Glad to hear that, sir."

"Yes. And so, I can promise you, the organization that lives on such hatred will not exist here in the future. I have the influence, and the power, to make certain of that."

"Glad to hear that, too."

"Mrs. Bannister, because we are speaking of this difficult subject, I must now take up a certain matter with you."

Oh oh, thought Nina.

What does he want with me?

"You must be cognizant of the fact that little goes on in Bay St. Lucy—or has gone on here—without my knowing it."

"I realize that."

"I received a telephone call yesterday from a member of the school board. I will not say which member. That is of no concern. He'd been approached by the principal of the elementary school, a Ms. Wickersley."

"Adelia. Yes."

"This woman was apparently quite concerned that you and your husband were in support of Mr. Cousins' guardianship of Miss Royale."

"Yes. She came to our house and told us as much."

"Apparently she was, up until yesterday evening, contacting school board members, urging that you be terminated."

"I'm not surprised."

"I am now informed though that Ms. Wickersley is leaving Bay St. Lucy."

Nina nodded.

"She thinks God sent the hurricane because of the town's acceptance of co-habitation."

"Which is absurd, of course."

"Well, Adelia Wickersley is an absurd woman."

"As well as being an ex-resident of Bay St. Lucy. The town will not suffer from her departure. Our high school though—and I promise you it will re-open, and it will do so in two months or less—will need a principal."

"Yes. And I'm sure there are a lot of people who—"

"It should be you."

She sat for a time in stunned disbelief.

And Goethe's words came back to her. The ones she'd always thought of when looking at Homer Baron Robinson:

Er will mich.

He wants me.

And now he did want her.

He continued:

"I believe I have enough influence with the board to make that happen."

"I'm—I'm so young—"

"Bay St. Lucy is young. It is, in fact, just beginning. Just as you will be. You and the town will be perfect for each other."

"I don't know. There's so much about being a principal that I know nothing about."

"Just think about it. That's all I ask."

"All right. I will."

"And now, back to what I was saying about Evelyn. She had a dream for Bay St. Lucy. And even though she will not be here and living with me in the future, I should like to do my part to make that dream a reality."

"She told me," said Nina, "that she wanted Bay St. Lucy to become an artist's colony."

"Yes. Those were her wishes exactly. And I think I can help to make that happen. Mr. Bannister?"

"Yes?"

"I believe that, with a good attorney helping me, I can purchase most of the highly damaged property in the downtown area. I then intend to rent it, for very reasonable sums, to painters, actors—people who love the beauty of the sea, and wish to use its powers to create more beauty. Surely there must be many such people."

And then it was Cousins' daughter who spoke up.

"There are, sir. And I know a lot of them. I know at least four people in New Orleans, and two more in New York, who'd come here tomorrow and help rebuild Bay St. Lucy, if they could be promised a chance to open shops here."

Nina immediately liked this young woman.

"Will you," she asked, "come here yourself?"

A nod.

"Yes. When I thought my father was dead, I realized what an idiot I'd been. I want to come here and live with him now. I have a new sister, Penelope; I have my father back—and I have a new home city. The artist colony of Bay St. Lucy."

"That's wonderful to hear," said Nina. "I want to be your first new friend in town. My name is Nina Bannister."

The woman stepped forward, and the two of them shook hands.

"I'm so happy to know you."

"And your name? It's not Cousins, I assume."

"No, I go by my married name now."

"And that is?"

"Delafosse. I'm Alanna Delafosse."

Within five minutes, they were walking out of the mansion, Frank with a new set of property work, Nina with a new friend and a possible new job, and Bay St. Lucy with a new vision for the future.

They were met just beyond the entrance by Moon Rivard's patrol car.

He rolled down the window and smiled up at them:

"I just got a call from the chief. He says Mr. Homer Baron Robinson talked with him, and asked that you be picked up."

"What," asked Frank, "did we do wrong?"

"Nothing! Why? Did you think you were being kidnapped?"

"It has," Nina said, quietly, "happened before."

"No, nothing like that. He just asked me to take all of you to the football field. The high school is just a shell of what it was, but the field has been cleared and they're bringing in portable buildings. I think there's probably free beds enough that you can all four sleep there tonight, and even take a shower if you want. Come on. Get in."

They did so, Frank beside Moon in the front seat, Lazarus, Alanna, and Nina in the back.

"Mr. Robinson," said Moon, pulling out onto the driveway, "has been a life saver. He called us as soon as the storm had passed and volunteered his grounds and his house. Kind of funny. I'd never known much about the man. Rumors were that he had gang connections in New Orleans and elsewhere. Always seemed kind of standoffish. But something changed him, I guess. Especially hard to imagine him doing all of this in light of his wife."

"He told us," Nina said quietly, "that she had gone."

Moon nodded.

"Yes, ma'am, that's true."

"How," Frank asked, "did she get out? He told us she'd left last night. But I thought the roads were closed."

Moon frowned:

"I'm not sure I understand you, Mr. Bannister."

Nina:

"Mr. Robinson said just now that his wife Evelyn had left him, that she'd gone away last night. But that was in the worst part of the storm. The roads were impassable. How did she get out of Bay St. Lucy?"

To which Moon answered, shaking his head, slowly:

"I don't think you understood him right, Ms. Bannister. Evelyn Robinson was in town last night, right in the worst of the storm, helping people get out of their flooded houses and into cars that were going over to the mansion. Several officers tried to warn her, get her to come back here herself. But she wouldn't stop. 'I've got to help them!' she kept saying. I was one of those officers. I heard her myself."

"But he said she left him!"

"She did leave him, Ms. Bannister. She was out in the town when the surge hit. So she left us all."

"You mean she—"

"Yes, Ms. Bannister. Evelyn Robinson is dead."

CHAPTER TWENTY FOUR: ALL THOSE IN PERIL ON THE SEA

Hurricane Camille killed 143 people on the Gulf Coast.

Twenty-two of these had been residents of Bay St. Lucy, where the worst of the storm surge had struck.

Sunday, seven days after the storm's landfall, a number of people gathered in the sanctuary of what had been the old First Methodist Church. The church's white steeple was gone, as were its red brick walls. But the basement walls were intact, and, after several days of intensive cleaning, a space had been created where worship was once again possible. There were seven rows of straight chairs, ten chairs in each row. The church's silver crucifix had been found, half a mile distant, lying upon one of the huge upturned blocks of concrete and asphalt that had once been a part of Breakers Boulevard.

It now stood atop a makeshift altar.

The group gathered in the church differed greatly, Nina Bannister noted from her seat in the farthest pew back, from the one that had gathered some days earlier to mourn for Eva Royale.

In that particular gathering there had been only white faces.

But the sea when angry is no respecter of race.

Nor is death.

And so Lazarus Cousins and his daughter Alanna Delafosse were not the only people in this crowd who'd come to mourn their deceased loved ones.

Hispanic, Asian, Indian—they were all present.

Hurricane Camille, with its monstrous and devastating power, had, if only for a moment, washed racial hatred from the village of Bay St. Lucy.

The minister delivered a small eulogy.

Small, for, as Nina had noted earlier, for the depths, of what use is language?

There were no song books in the cellar-church, of course. But the people gathered there—and the space was full—knew the song that led off the service, for they were people who lived by and upon the sea.

Eternal Father, strong to save,
Whose arm hath bound the restless wave,
Who bid'st the mighty ocean deep
Its own appointed limits keep;
Oh, hear us when we cry to Thee,
For those in peril on the sea!
O Christ! Whose voice the waters heard
And hushed their raging at Thy word,
Who walked'st on the foaming deep,
And calm amidst its rage didst sleep;
Oh, hear us when we cry to Thee,
For those in peril on the sea!
Most Holy Spirit! Who didst brood
Upon the chaos dark and rude,
And bid its angry tumult cease,
And give, for wild confusion, peace;
Oh, hear us when we cry to Thee,
For those in peril on the sea!
O Trinity of love and power!
Our brethren shield in danger's hour;
From rock and tempest, fire and foe,
Protect them wheresoe'er they go;
Thus evermore shall rise to Thee
Glad hymns of praise from land and sea.

After the last verse of the song had been completed there was silence for a time in the church.

Then, as time and tradition had taught it to do, the group repeated two lines:

Oh, hear us when we cry to Thee
For those in peril on the sea!

After singing which, the group dispersed.

Nina, Frank by her side, found Homer Baron Robinson standing beside his black limousine, preparing to get in and slide behind the wheel. He had no driver.

His white face had been stained, like a clean handkerchief is darkened in spots by water droplets.

He managed a handshake with both of them, though only a weak smile.

"Your children?" asked Nina.

"With acquaintances. In New Orleans. They shall return tomorrow. I need them here."

Silence for a time.

"A beautiful service," he said, quietly.

Nina:

"She would have liked it, Mr. Robinson."

He nodded, then replied:

"They all would have."

To which, Frank said:

"Perhaps they all did."

Nina:

"I've thought over what you asked me, about being principal."

"And your decision?"

"I'll do it. I'll be the best principal of Bay St. Lucy High School that I can be. But only under one condition."

"That being?"

"Send your children to school here. We may not have the best educational facilities in the world. But we're all a community. Especially now."

He nodded.

"You're right. They will be there."

They said a few more words, then he got into the car and drove off.

And so, after a time, Nina and Frank were left alone, standing in front of the church, looking out over the field of rubble that had been Bay St. Lucy.

People were wandering about, some carrying bundles of clothing, others simply looking as though they had no particular direction in which to walk.

Nina, ever the English teacher, said softly:

Som natural tears they drop'd, but wip'd them soon;
[645]
The World was all before them,
and Providence thir guide:
They hand in hand with wandring steps and slow,
Through *Eden* took thir solitarie way.

"*Paradise Lost*?" Frank asked.

"Yes."

"Do you think, Nina, that our paradise is lost?"

She shook her head and replied.

"Give me your hand, Frank."

He did so, and she gripped it, strongly:

"I think we'll live through *Paradise Regained*, Frank. Whatever happens, though, as long as we love each other the way we do—and we'll love each other that way for as long as we live—Bay St. Lucy will be our *Treasure Island*. Now let's go home."

And they did.

EPILOGUE

Bay St. Lucy, a little kaleidoscope Mississippi village on the Gulf Coast. Red board building here, bright blue shack there, lighthouse in the distance, dog over by the fire plug, squirrel in the tree—all there in front of her, above her, surrounding her, just waiting to be gobbled up by her senses and devoured by her beingness.

And so Nina Bannister savored it as she opened the door of her battered Volkswagen and got out, stretching for a moment, listening to the ocean which was no more than half a mile distant, and letting her eyes scan the town around her.

Construction everywhere, with business being transacted in portable buildings and even tents, while trucks brought in building materials and took out the debris that was still being collected.

Square pasteboard signs nailed upon posts and tree trunks and walls and fences, all of the signs saying the same thing:

THE GULF COAST WILL RISE AGAIN!

She checked her watch: twelve fifteen.

She had, due to the fact that she was a new principal who understood coffee and cream and young love—and would never be persuaded that such things did not exist—forty five more minutes.

And so she slammed shut the door of the car with somewhat more force than might have been absolutely necessary, causing, as it did, the entire vehicle to shudder somewhat. Then she strode off across the broad, red-clay roadbed on which concrete was to be poured the following week, thus creating the new Breakers Boulevard.

Soon the corrugated iron building she'd been approaching stood before her, the step-up cinder block beneath her feet, the buzzer at hand, and the click-lock negotiated.

Raaack!

The door swung open to reveal a tall young mop-haired man in a shirt that was not quite as right as the hastily erected building itself.

"Hey!" this young man shouted, his face illuminating like a fall carnival on a Friday night.

"Hey!" she responded. "How's the morning? Are we rich and famous yet?"

"Give me until this afternoon!"

"You keep saying that. I'm disappointed."

"So no hug?"

"I didn't say that."

And then they were, deliciously, embracing.

Which they did for far too long, given the forty-three minutes and twelve—now eleven now ten now nine etc etc etc seconds they still had to be together before she returned to the high school.

But at the end, they unembraced, and that was not too bad either, for they were now standing at arm's length from each other, with just the right spacing so that she could look up at him—she was short and he was tall—and say:

"I love you, Frank Bannister."

"I love you, Nina Bannister. So let's have lunch!"

And they did.

And it was a beautiful day in mid-October.

And the morning was like cream.

NOTES

Homer Baron Robinson was murdered three years later in his home. The assassins were thought to be drug runners working out of New Orleans, but they were never caught. Details concerning the murder can be found in the novel *Sea Change: A Nina Bannister Mystery.*

Penelope Royale continued to live with Lazarus Cousins until his death in 1983. She continues today to run one of Bay St. Lucy's favorite charter fishing services.

Alanna Delafosse took up residence in Bay St. Lucy, working tirelessly for the development of the artistic community. In 2014, she became curator of the Auberge des Arts, in the same building that had once been known as the Robinson Mansion.

Hope and Paul Reddington's son, Tommy, eleven years old in 1969, married Estelle Farmer in 1980. Four years later, their daughter Helen Reddington was born. In 1990, Tommy and Estelle died in an automobile accident. Hope, by then a widow herself, raised the girl. Helen became a Shakespearian actress in New York City. Her return to Bay St. Lucy to star as Ophelia in a world class production of *Hamlet* is described in the novel *Set Change: A Nina Bannister Mystery.*

Moon Rivard became the Chief of Police in Bay St. Lucy, and still holds that position today, although he has long since passed retirement age.

Judge Richard Davis, attempting to save records from the county courthouse, was swept up in Camille's storm surge, and drowned.

Evelyn Robinson drowned likewise, while attempted to save two children, who'd taken refuge on the roof of their house trailer.

Nina Bannister spent her entire career as principal of Bay St. Lucy High School, retiring in the year 2005 at the age of sixty. She and her husband Frank, who passed away in 2004, remained childless. She returned to service as high school principal in 2014, and also coached the Bay St. Lucy women's basketball team to a regional championship. Half a year later, she was elected to fill a congressional seat made vacant by the tragic airline death of a popular state legislator. The details concerning these events can be read in the novels *Game Change: A Nina Bannister Mystery* and *Sex Change: A Nina Bannister Mystery.*

The Ku Klux Klan was never seen again in the thriving artist community that is now Bay St. Lucy

THE END

ABOUT THE AUTHORS

 Pam Britton (T'Gracie) Reese is an Assistant Professor in the Communication Science and Disorders Department at Indiana/Purdue University at Fort Wayne. Previously, she worked as a speech pathologist in schools in private practice. She was also a supervisor in communication disorders at Ohio University. She likes nothing better, professionally, than helping small, silent two-year-old boys start talking. She has also published books about autism with LinguiSystems for the last 15 years. *The Circle of Autism* was previously published online at *ken*again e-magazine.*

Joe Reese is a novelist, playwright, storyteller, and college teacher. He has published four novels, several plays, and a number of stories and articles. When he's not teaching (English and German), he enjoys visiting elementary schools, where he tells stories from his Katie Dee novels and talks to students about writing. He and his wife Pam have three children: Kate, Matthew, and Sam.

OTHER BOOKS BY T'GRACIE AND JOE REESE:

Sea Change
Set Change
Game Change
Oil Change
Frame Change
Sex Change
Climate Change
Mind Change

www.ingramcontent.com/pod-product-compliance
Lightning Source LLC
Chambersburg PA
CBHW050409260626
47156CB00003B/941